Jim has written short stories for various publications in Ireland. He got first prize in the golden pen short story competition in 2003. Another short story by Jim, *Lost Love*, was adapted into a film by an independent film company in the UK. A screenplay based on the story was written by director Rosita Clarke called, *The Other Side of the Lake*. He played a part in the film. It won an award for best director in the Ladies first International film festival in Cork in 2017. In 2020 the film won an award for best editing of a feature film at the London International film festival. In the same year it won an award for best original screenplay at the Nice International film festival. Jim lives in Dublin with his wife and family. His interests are writing, acting, reading and history.

To my wife Phil and daughters Anna and Zita. Thank you for your support.

Jim Burke

THE SAD WINDOWS

AUSTIN MACAULEY PUBLISHERS™
LONDON • CAMBRIDGE • NEW YORK • SHARJAH

A CIP catalogue record for this title is available from the British Library.

ISBN 9781528993166 (Paperback)
ISBN 9781528993173 (ePub e-book)

www.austinmacauley.com

First Published (2020)
Austin Macauley Publishers Ltd
25 Canada Square
Canary Wharf
London
E14 5LQ

Thank you to my parents and my family. My father inspired me with his tales of the supernatural over the years. Also, thanks to Austin Macauley Publishers for their help with the publication of this book.

Chapter 1

The sight of the house amazed me. It was huge and I felt tiny standing in front of it on that dark cloudy Friday in October 1929. I'd never been this close to it before. The high corinthian portico was held up by six granite columns. The grey stone had become green in places from the weather over the many years that it had stood there. Marble statues of fierce looking lions flanked both sides to the entrance. I touched one of them and it felt cold and smooth. The windows were long and had an air of melancholy about them. To me, they looked as if they were crying, and I imagined how miserable they must have looked when the rain ran down their panes. I had been asked to a special birthday party at the house. It was Ellen Rackley's 21st and she wanted all her friends there. I was delighted to go for two reasons. The first was being asked in the first place and getting a chance to maybe dance with Ellen and see inside the mansion that she called home. The second was because I liked Ellen, but I wasn't under any illusions about her or I being together or as anything more than good friends. We were from different backgrounds. I did like her though, more than liked her, and I knew she liked me. We'd known each other all our lives and we belonged to a large circle of friends. I liked to think I had a place in Ellen's heart. There were times when she made me feel special, but we'd never gone out together. I went on dates with other girls and they came and went. With Ellen, it was the same and she too had lots of dates. She was always very popular, but I don't think she cared too much about popularity. I once overheard her saying that she didn't care what people thought of her. She just wanted to be liked for who she was, nothing else.

As I stood at the entrance to her home, all these thoughts passed through my mind. I pulled the bell cord beside the front door and heard it ringing somewhere down the hallway. While waiting to be admitted, I thought I heard the faint faraway strains of orchestral music coming from somewhere in the house. It seemed to be emanating from someplace over my head. I could tell it wasn't a gramophone; it didn't have that scratching sound. I stepped back from the door and looked up at one of the sad windows on the next floor. There was a young woman with a pale face, dark hair, and penetrating eyes looking back at me. She was wearing a white bonnet with a yellow ribbon which partly shaded her face. She raised her hand as if to block the remaining daylight from her eyes. I thought this unusual as there was hardly any light left and it was almost dark. My eyes remained on her and try as I may, I couldn't divert them. I was fixed to the spot and to the face behind the glass. It was as though I was in a trance. Suddenly, she was gone and the spell was broken. I didn't recognise her and I stood there wondering if I'd imagined her; the music had stopped also. I don't know why, but I felt a shudder going across my shoulders. It was like a feeling of impending doom. I felt frightened or shocked or taken by surprise. I didn't know what I felt. There was something other worldly about the face. A strong wind started to rise and the nearby trees in the surrounding grounds began to wave their branches in an ominous kind of motion, like giant hands. I didn't get time to think more about the face, as the door creaked open and a man aged about fifty dressed in a black suit with a white shirt and black bow tie stood in front of me.

"I'm here for the party, I'm John Wilson. Ellen is expecting me," I said feeling nervous before him.

"Please come in sir and I'll show you the way."

I followed him and he shut the door after me, it made a booming sound in the large arched hallway.

"Let me take your coat," he said in a rather stiff way. I handed it to him and he hung it on a huge mahogany coat rack that stood in the corner with deer antlers for hooks. A grandfather clock stood against the wall. Its swinging pendulum and slow tick tock caught my attention. If ever an item of furniture fitted in with its surroundings, the clock did. It belonged to a world of long ago, a world of a slower pace. I looked around me, taking everything in. I couldn't hear any orchestral music. I'd never been in a house like this before and never expected to be either, unless on some sort of tour. There were several paintings on the walls. I imagined them to be ancestors of Ellen and wondered what they were like when they too lived here. I was going to ask the butler if he knew who was who, but there was something forbidding in the look he gave me. He motioned slowly with his white-gloved hand for me to follow him. As I walked, my shoes made a horrible squeaking noise on the black and white tiled floor. I felt myself cringing with embarrassment but thankfully he never looked back or said anything. *A perfect gentleman,* I thought to myself. It seemed a long walk to where he was leading me and I was glad when the tiles came to an end and we were walking on carpet.

"Are there many other people here yet?" I asked as I followed him along.

"You're the first one sir. The party is for 6 p.m." I wondered why I was there at 5 p.m. as that had been the time I was given.

We arrived at a dark wooden door which was inset and knocking, he turned the brass doorknob at the same time.

"Mr John Wilson, my lady."

Ellen ran towards me and the man in black left, closing the door behind him. It made an echoing sound.

"John, John, thank you for coming, oh and look you've brought me a present, how kind you are." She put her arms around me and kissed me on the cheek. She looked lovely in a long white dress that was low off the shoulders with a large bow at the back. Her dark brown hair were up and there were three star-like hairclips on her head, keeping the hair in place. I sat down on the sofa and she sat beside me. She put her hand on mine and thanked me again for coming. I asked if it was her face that I'd seen at the window. I knew it wasn't but I couldn't figure out who it was. She looked irritated and I just knew I'd said something that she didn't want to hear.

"No," she replied sharply, "I've been here downstairs all day. There's nobody here except you, me, and Dillon, the butler. My mother and father will be back soon with my brothers and sisters. The other staff members have gone to the village. They'll be back in time to help start feeding us. So, you see, you must have been imagining things."

I wasn't convinced.

"If my eyes were deceiving me, my ears weren't. You must have heard the music." She looked as though she was very cross with me.

"No," she said, "I didn't and would you stop asking me questions on my birthday. You've only just arrived and all these questions. Our friends will be here soon and I want us to enjoy ourselves. Sometimes draughts through keyholes make a musical sound."

I felt I had to agree; I didn't want to upset her on her birthday.

She opened the present and loved it. I'd got her a silver bracelet and she put it on immediately.

"Oh, it's lovely and you've got it inscribed, 'To Ellen with love John'." I thought I saw a tear in her eye. I stood up and embraced her. She kissed me on the cheek again.

"Don't cry," I said, "it's supposed to make you smile." She walked over to the door and after opening it looked out into the corridor. She closed it again and came back.

"Sit down," she said in a low voice. "I'm sorry if I snapped at you. There's something I want to tell you and that's the reason I asked you to come early. When you came in just now, I felt happy and decided to forget about telling you. When you asked me about the face at the window and the sounds of music, I felt annoyed. It was because I realised there's no getting away from it. I don't want anyone else to know." I looked at her with growing curiosity.

"This sounds strange," I said. "You're not under any threat, are you? For goodness sake Ellen, what are you trying to say?" A look of fear came into her eyes and I imagined I could hear her heartbeat thumping faster and faster.

"All right," she began, "yes, I've heard sounds that I can't account for. I didn't want to say it at first when you mentioned it, but yes; music and whispering. I'm upset even talking about it. I've tried to bring it up with my parents but they just shrug it off and put it down to my imagination. It's only recently that I've noticed it." Her eyes started to water again.

"Please Ellen," I said. "Don't cry, let me be your confidante and close friend. Your guests will be arriving soon and you're going to have a nice time on your special birthday. We can talk about this later or even at another time." She put her head on my shoulder. I could sense her fear.

"Yes, you're right," she said lifting her head quickly and becoming more cheerful, "we'll talk about it later but in the meantime let's enjoy my party. I heard you're working in a bookshop; do you like it?" I told her I did and that at some stage I would give some thought to teaching about books rather than selling them. The conversation continued like that, talking about everything except that which was troubling her. I made up my mind I would say nothing more about it unless she wanted to.

The hour passed quickly and the party started. Ellen's parents were there along with her friends. Her sisters, Mary and Caroline, were there also with her brothers, Tony and Billy. I observed them as the evening went on and I could tell they were a close family. I found Tony and Billy nice to talk with and good listeners. Mary and Caroline were the same. Ellen seemed to have forgotten our earlier conversation and was having a wonderful time. I talked to my friends, most of whom I'd known all my life. We'd all gone to school and college together and were now making our way in life. I was working in a bookshop in the village and I loved it. I had studied literature in college and was qualified to teach it. At that time in my life, I wanted to work in a bookshop and I'd got a job in one known as the tell-tale.

"Come and meet my parents, John." Ellen was dragging me over to talk with her folks and I felt shy as I'd never met them. I'd seen them before but had never spoken to them.

"John, say hello to my parents." I shook their hands and they too seemed friendly. Her father was a jovial kind of man but at the same time a no-nonsense kind of person. He liked to talk and had a habit of looking at the end of his nose as he spoke. Ellen's mother was just as talkative, even more, so it was hard to get a word in. They asked me the usual questions; where I worked, where I lived, how long I knew Ellen, and so on. I couldn't decide if they were assessing me or were indeed just being friendly. I decided on the later; I hoped I was right.

The time came for the cake to be brought out. Ellen's father said a few nice words and thanked everybody for being there. Mrs Rackley urged everyone to eat drink and be merry. This was followed by a cheer and then there was a call for Ellen to say something. I could see her turning red at first and then growing very pale. Her natural colour returned slowly and she stood beside her sister, Mary, holding her hand.

"Thank you," she began, "everybody for coming to my birthday party. I'm enjoying myself immensely and hope all of you are too. Thank you for the lovely presents. We've got a large room upstairs with a piano and a gramophone and I fancy dancing into the early hours. What do you say?"

Somebody shouted from the back, "Let's see this room." This was followed by cheers and laughter.

"Don't worry, you'll see the room soon enough," she replied.

"When we have our cake and some tea and when I hear the clock striking twelve, we make our way up." I looked at her and saw how happy she was there amongst friends and family and being the centre of attention. I felt happy too, happy that she was happy. Just for a moment I found myself wondering what the future held for her and for me too. I turned in the direction of the drinks and a few seconds later I felt a tap on my shoulder. I turned around and Ellen was offering me a slice of cake on a small plate. I took it from her and she smiled.

"Will you stay on," she asked, "I mean really late if I ask you to?"

"I'll stay all night if you find me somewhere to sleep. Tomorrow is Saturday and so I don't have to be up early." I could see she was happy with my answer and she moved off to talk to some of the others. I watched her as she spoke with them and I felt I was falling under a spell she was casting, a spell I was more than happy to fall under. Her smile lit up the room and I felt in love.

I got some more cake and was talking to Michael Maguire, an old schoolmate of mine. He was telling me what he was doing with himself and how he was now engaged to be married.

"Susan is here come over and say hello." I crossed the room and he introduced us. She was a friendly girl, pretty with dimples. As I was shaking her hand, I got a strange feeling that someone was watching me. I looked past Susan. Through the open doorway I saw or thought I saw, the young woman I'd seen at the window when I'd first called. She seemed almost translucent. Her face now wore a cruel expression. Suddenly, she was gone. I must have turned pale because Michael was asking me, was I feeling alright.

"You just seemed to drift off there for a few seconds and went white, are you sure you're okay?"

"It must have been the cake, my tummy felt a little bit off, I'm okay now thanks."

Ellen must have sensed something because she came over and asked me if I was okay.

"I'm fine," I replied, "really I am, please don't trouble yourself."

Later in the night, I heard the clock chime twelve and we were led by Ellen to the room with the piano and gramophone. On the way up the oak stairway I felt strange. I wondered was it a ghost I'd seen earlier and the feeling I felt afterwards was like nothing I'd ever felt before. I could only describe it as a kind of lost-empty and at the same time, a frightening feeling. I couldn't help noticing the beautiful blue stained-glass skylight over the stairs. It depicted a pastoral scene. It

15

reminded me of one of Constable's paintings. I thought to myself, as we all shuffled up the stairs and along the gallery, *how nice it would be to live in this beautiful house.* I wasn't going to say what I'd seen to Ellen. I wanted so badly not to upset her.

She brought us to the room and two servants were serving sandwiches and tea along with stronger drinks. The walls of the room were painted dark blue and there was a magnificent ornate ceiling. The grand piano stood in the centre of the room and there was a gramophone on a small table nearby. Both were highly polished.

"Get more tea and food and drinks or whatever you want," said Ellen. She proceeded to wind up the gramophone and the music started. Everyone put down their glasses and took to the floor. I asked Kate Dempsey to join me on the floor. Kate was always friendly and we'd gone out together in the past. I liked her very much at the time but our relationship fizzled out. I had missed her a lot, but I was over it now. She had come with her brother, Tommy. We danced and she told me what she'd been doing with herself since.

"I'm working in an insurance office and I like it," she said, "it's busy and every Friday, Mark comes and collects me in his car."

"Oh, who's Mark?" I asked.

"He's my boyfriend. He couldn't come, but he wanted me to have a good time with my friends. Is it true that we're all staying tonight? How thrilling it would be to stay in one of these houses."

"I don't know for sure," I replied. "I think we can come or go if we want." I tried to imagine what Mark was like. He'd got somebody nice in Kate. She moved away and started talking to some of the others.

"Are you enjoying yourself?" It was Ellen's voice. I hadn't heard her coming up behind me. She was smoking a cigarette in one those long cigarette holders.

"I didn't know you smoked."

"I don't," she answered. "It's just for fun at a party when I have one and tonight, I feel like one." I liked her casual demeanour at that present moment. It wasn't always the impression she gave, indeed a few hours earlier I had seen her very differently. She smiled and looked at me and at the bracelet.

"I must mingle. I'll talk to you later," she said smiling and tapped me on the arm.

Later, everybody was lying on cushions and on a few armchairs and sofas that were around the room. Most, if not all of them had fallen asleep. I tried to keep my eyes open, but I eventually nodded off. Somewhere in the middle of a dream that involved me being chased, by whom I couldn't say, I suddenly woke. The room was chilly and everything was quiet except for the noise of the gramophone needle stuck on the record. I rose slowly and walked over to release it, nearly tripping on an empty bottle. I lifted the arm free and the terrible scratching stopped.

"What time is it?" came Ellen's voice behind me.

"It's three in the morning," I whispered, "keep your voice down, let them sleep." She asked me if I'd like some tea, but that we'd have to make it ourselves as all the staff would be in bed now. I told her I'd love some. What happened next was very strange. We were standing beside the piano about to make our way to the kitchen when suddenly, two notes were played. Ellen went white and looked at me. I felt a shiver from the top of my head, all the way down my back. We continued to stand there looking at each other. Ellen was the first to speak.

"What does it mean, what's happening? You heard it too, didn't you?"

"Yes!" I said turning and staring at my reflection in the shining surface of the piano. "Come on let's get that tea."

Chapter 2

I followed her downstairs and along a flag stoned passageway that led to a green door with the words 'servants hall' painted on it in large white letters. We entered a big kitchen area with a high ceiling. It had a shining black range and around the walls were lots of wide presses and shelves. The range hadn't quite gone out so there was still a little bit of heat in the room. There was a long table in the centre of the kitchen, covered up with a huge green and white tablecloth. Twelve very straight wooden chairs were placed around it. I thought of the last supper. There was a line of bells with coils attached over the door. Under each one was the name of the room to where the bell was connected. I thought how busy a place it must have been during the day but now it was deadly quiet.

"You definitely heard the piano playing, didn't you?" Ellen asked, as she placed two white mugs with blue rims on the table. "I mean I'm not going mad, am I?"

"Yes!" I replied, "I heard it but saw no one playing. I can't explain it, Ellen, pianos don't usually play by themselves." She didn't say anything further and got the tea from the range. A minute later we were drinking tea and sitting in the kitchen that was now growing colder and colder. I saw her shivering and gave her my jacket to put over her bare shoulders. She thanked me and gave me that magical smile that only she could give. It was a smile people would kill for. I lit a cigarette; I always liked a smoke with a cup of tea and sat in an old floral-patterned armchair in front of the homely range watching the blue smoke disappearing into the atmosphere.

"I'll think I'll join you for a smoke," she said and from some sort of hidden side pocket in her dress, she drew out the long cigarette holder that I'd seen her with earlier.

"Sorry," I said, "I forgot you liked the occasional one." She took one from the cigarette case that I offered her and put it into the holder. We laughed as she placed the long contraption in her mouth. I flicked the lighter and the flame lit up her face.

"Thank you," she said, "that's a nice lighter you have there."

"Would you believe I won it at one of those seaside carnivals?"

"That's gas," she said pouring the tea from a white delph teapot, "I like those places. We better drink this while it's still hot." She sat opposite me and for a moment nothing was said. All around us the house was silent except, now and again, we heard the movement of coal in the stove as it shifted and turned to ash. Thankfully we didn't hear the piano playing by itself again. I wondered what the explanation for it was. Since I'd come to the house, I'd wondered about a lot of things. The quietness was striking. It was wrong what people said about silence being golden, even it has a sound, a kind of low ringing in the ears.

"Wasn't it nice of Mary, our housekeeper, to have some tea made for us before she went to bed," said Ellen, "she often does that if she thinks we're going to be late home. She's such a dear." I looked at her as she spoke these words and thought what a nice thing for her to say. Things like that meant a lot to me and still do. It was pleasant to be sitting in that kitchen, just the two of us. There was nowhere else I wanted to be at that very moment.

"You will stay for breakfast, won't you?" she asked.

"Yes, I'd like that once it's not too early," I joked. She looked at me and I felt that she was searching for something else to talk about. I could tell she still felt uncomfortable about the piano incident, a face at the window, music playing, and whispering.

"How do you like working in the bookshop?" she asked suddenly, as if trying hard to distract herself.

"It's okay, I'm enjoying it. I'm glad tomorrow is Saturday; I don't how I'd get through the day. You should come in some time, maybe I could get you to buy a book."

"Fancy yourself as a good salesman, do you?" she asked smiling. I told her I'd sold quite a few books since I'd started to work there. She smiled again and then suddenly stopped.

"I'm going away on Wednesday for two weeks," she said. I was taken completely by surprise.

"Where to?" I asked.

"I'm going to cousins of mine who live in Germany. They've been asking me for ages to come so I'm off on Wednesday. I'm looking forward to a change of scenery. I will come back though, to help manage the estate here so you needn't look so glum, you've not seen the last of me. Maybe I'll get a job in that bookshop of yours!" I felt disappointed that she was going away at all and obviously it showed on my face.

"What about you, are you happy with your lot?" she asked.

"I'm enjoying selling books in the shop, but I'd like to start teaching about them some day. I don't feel ready for that yet. I get a kick out of watching people buying and reading them. There'll be plenty of time, I suppose, in the future for the more serious stuff of explaining them rather than selling them."

"Why don't you feel ready now?" she asked with an inquisitive look on her face. I hesitated and she didn't wait for an answer.

"What do you say we go back up and join the others? I've arranged for us to be called about nine in the morning or should I say in a few hours," she said starting to look tired.

"You have a lovely smile, but I bet I'm not the first person to tell you that," I said looking into her eyes.

"Did anyone ever tell you that you have very insightful eyes, eyes that look deep into a person's soul," she replied.

We smiled at each other. Suddenly I noticed her face change and I knew other thoughts were going through her mind.

"What is it?" I asked.

"I feel a bit frightened tonight, not just tonight. What or why are these strange things happening? I know it sounds foolish, but I even feel too afraid to sleep. To be honest I wish you could stay in my room, but I couldn't risk my parents finding out about my secret stowaway. Oh, don't mind me, I'll be alright. In a way I wish I wasn't going away and yet I'm looking forward to a break from this old house and whatever it is that's here." She spoke rapidly and I told her I would always look out for her and be there for her.

"Well that's enough for me. Are you tired? Do you want to go to your bed now?" she asked.

"In a minute. I don't want to leave this kitchen, it's cosy just the two of us chatting here. I love sitting up late at night sometimes, but it's usually alone without good company to talk to. Do you intend to live here in the future?"

"Yes!" she replied, "Well that is maybe until I get my own place. I do have a strong attachment to it though so perhaps I'll never leave. Do you feel the same about where you live?" I told her I did but at the same time would not find it difficult to leave. She stood up and raked through the ashes with a poker but the range had almost gone out completely. I thought she looked lonely or frightened, a kind of haunted look. I too felt uneasy for her and what it was that might be frightening her. I felt sorry for myself also that she would be away for two weeks. I was in love.

The kitchen was very cold at this stage and we both shivered. Ellen yawned and looked at me with heavy eyelids.

"Okay," I said, "it's time to go to bed before we die from the cold." She stood up without any question and put her arm into mine, linking me with her.

"It's a long way back to the others, I might get lost," she joked.

"You don't need an excuse to take my arm, anytime," I said softly.

"Do you really mean that?"

"Yes, I wouldn't say it if I didn't." We walked in the direction of the stairs and suddenly she stopped.

"I'm not going to delay you anymore from getting some sleep," she said, "but please give me your word that you won't discuss with anybody what we were talking about earlier or about the piano." I assured her I wouldn't and she pressed my arm.

"Good, now your room is at the far end of the gallery. It's got a blue and white vase outside and a picture of a lake hanging above it."

"My own room indeed, so I don't have to sleep on the floor, very nice thank you."

She pointed out the direction of the room I was to stay in and then took her leave of me to return to her own room but not before kissing me first. This time it was not on the cheek. She followed this with a quick goodnight and was gone in another direction without looking back. I watched her disappearing into the darkness. I proceeded on in the direction she had told me to go. I found the room and went in, closing the door behind me. A feeling of being cut off mixed with a miserable feeling came over me. I couldn't work out why I felt like this, it was so sudden. I hadn't been feeling unhappy, it just seemed to happen as soon as I shut the door. I told myself that I was being far too sensitive. Electric light had been fitted and I flicked on the switch of the lamp on the table. I hoped the light from it would dispel the dark mood. I sat down in a red easy chair and stared at the pattern on the quilt. I wasn't admiring or taking it in but rather just staring and thinking of everything. This was a habit of mine when I found myself alone. After what seemed an age, I undressed and slid between the sheets. The bed felt fresh, if a little cold. I looked around and saw a large dark gloomy looking wardrobe on one side of the room and a small bookshelf on the other. I couldn't shake off the downhearted feeling and I got back out of bed to look at the books. It was a varied collection of novels and some old school books. They were dusty so I could tell they hadn't been looked at for a while. I sat on the bed and read the first two pages of a novel about wizards and magic. I yawned after a few minutes and put it back on the shelf. Ellen's face came into my mind again and just for a moment I imagined her in the room with me. It was a nice thought, but I thought it better not to torment myself and tried to forget about her. I got back into bed again and turned the light off. As I lay waiting for sleep to overcome me, I found myself picturing the face of the young woman that I'd seen at the window. I felt a strange frightened feeling rising within me and sat up quickly, turning the lamp on. I listened to the sound of silence and my heart thumping. I turned the light off again and eventually I sensed sleep coming over me. Somewhere not far from where I was, I could hear crying. I got out of bed again and opened the door. It was very dark and the crying stopped suddenly. I closed the door and got back into bed again. I heard the rain lightly hitting the window. Just before I fell asleep, I got the strongest feeling that I would never be lonely again.

Chapter 3

I rose early the next morning having been awakened by the stir downstairs. I washed, got dressed, and followed the smell of food which was now wafting in my direction. Coming down the stairs, I felt a little bit groggy from the night before, but I was a lot better than some of them there from what I could see. I found the breakfast room and sat down to orange juice followed by fried eggs, bacon, sausage and many cups of tea. There was a lot of tired looking faces all around the table and tea was in great demand; I don't know how many times I saw fresh pots of it being placed on the table. I couldn't see Ellen anywhere. Mrs Rackley came in and asked everybody if they'd slept well and had enough to eat. It seemed they had and just before she left the room, she came over to me with an envelope.

"Ellen had to rush into town this morning and asked me to give you this note. She won't be back until the afternoon," she said quietly handing me the envelope. She then walked off in the direction of the stairs.

"Well—well who's getting a private note from the birthday girl," said Michael Maguire trying to pull it out of my hand. I got on well with Michael, but I didn't feel like his antics first thing in the morning. I wanted to go somewhere quiet and read it. I ignored him and finished my breakfast. Most people were already finished and were staring to make their way home. A short time later I said my goodbyes to Ellen's family and closed the heavy front door behind me. Michael and Susan drove up in their little black car and asked me if I wanted a lift.

"No, you're okay, I feel like a walk and then I'll get the bus, thanks anyway." They waved and drove off. I waited until they'd gone from sight and then walked in among the trees and sat down on one that had fallen to read Ellen's note. I opened the envelope and took out the folded piece of paper. A faint scent of perfume greeted me. I unfolded it and read.

Dear John,

I had to rush off to town this morning. I remembered I had an appointment. Last night, after I went to bed, I heard noises. I sat up and listened and it was coming from the storeroom which is three doors away from my room. I got out of bed, threw on my dressing gown and went to see what the noise was. It used to be a nursery many years ago. The door wasn't locked so I went in. It was very dusty with a lot of old rubbish and some toys from long ago. They didn't interest me, but I found a tin box opened with documents in it. John, I have discovered something in the documents. I'll tell you more when I see you. It might throw some light on the strange events that we've both experienced lately. I might telephone you later.

Thank you again so much for the beautiful bracelet.

Ellen.

I looked at the note again especially the part where she thanked me for the bracelet. I felt connected to her. I put it in my pocket and walked down to the front gates and out on to the road. Rain was beginning to fall and I stood under a tree for shelter. The bus came after a few minutes and I went upstairs and sat in the front seat. There was a man on the inside and he appeared to be asleep. I didn't feel like having anyone near me at that moment except Ellen. I just wanted some alone time with her. I wanted to be involved in whatever it was that was causing her all this unrest. As the bus bumped and jerked along, I thought of when I'd first met Ellen. We were only children, but we got on so well together. We were brought to children's parties and it went on from there. It didn't matter to her or to us that we were from different backgrounds. Ellen made friends with us all and us with her. We were a circle of close friends and we did everything together. Now that we were finished with school and parties, we didn't get to see each other as much as before. 21st birthdays were coming around and we were being thrown together again. I liked it, liked it very much. I was working in the bookshop, making a steady wage, but I felt not quite content. I was living at home with my family but wanted my own place. Secretly, I used to imagine myself living in Ellen Rackley's house with big grounds to walk around in.

I got off the bus at my stop which was just at the top of the street where I lived. The rain had eased off as I walked in the direction of home. I glanced at the houses along our street as I passed by. I'd never really taken note of them before. They were homely, quaint really. People took pride in their gardens and indeed my father did too. Most Saturday mornings, in the summer, he would be found pottering around in the garden dressed in an old shop coat and straw hat. My mother loved the garden too and she was for ever planting flowers. The gate made a noise as I opened it, she turned in my direction.

"Ah, you're back. How was the party?"

"It was very nice. Ellen really enjoyed herself and she got a lot of nice presents. I got my breakfast before I left this morning. The flowers look lovely."

"Winter pansies but never mind the flowers," said my mother. "How did you get on?" I must have looked blankly at her because in a moment my father came to my rescue.

"Your mother means are we going to have the girl coming here for tea." He winked at me.

"I don't know, look I just went to a party and enjoyed myself. Don't be seeing things where there isn't anything."

"Ellen Rackley has always had a soft spot for you," said my mother. I looked at them both standing there among the pots and moss peat, hoping to get some information out of me.

"Why don't we all have a cup of tea," said my mother. "John, you go and put the kettle on." I was glad to and to get away from all the questions.

I soon had the kettle on and got out the cups and some biscuits. My parents came in and sat down. I poured the tea. Suddenly, my father stood up again and looked out the window. He pulled back the curtain to get a better look.

"You have a visitor John, Ellen Rackley, and she's just in time for a cup of tea." He did his mischievous wink at my mother as he said this. The doorbell rang and I walked quickly to the door. I could see her shape through the frosted glass. I opened the door and we looked directly at each other.

"I hope, I'm not intruding John," she said in a low voice, "but I have something here you might be interested in. I couldn't wait any longer before showing you." She opened her handbag and showed me a yellowing document; well it was more of a collection of papers that smelt musty. They were held together by a large clip.

"I wasn't expecting to see you for two weeks. Come in," I said. "You can meet Mam and Dad. We're just about to have a cup of tea and some biscuits. You haven't seen them since school." She came into the hall and I hung up her coat. She looked in the mirror to check her hair. We went into the kitchen and my parents were delighted to see her.

"Ellen, this is Mam and Dad."

"It's lovely to meet you both. I have met you before as you know but it's been a long time," said Ellen.

"It has indeed," said my mother, "too long. You were in school. I know you run into John from time to time, he sometimes lets us know how you are. You'll join us in the sitting room for some tea and biscuits. John bring Ellen into the sitting room and we'll be in in a minute." I showed her the way and we sat on the sofa. It felt nice to have her in my home.

"Is that the discovery that you mentioned in your note?" I asked pointing to her bag.

"Yes, just wait and see what it says." She was excited with this news. I wondered how it was connected to the face at the window, the orchestral music, and the piano playing by itself.

I didn't get a chance to find out as my parents came in. My mother was carrying a tray of tea and biscuits and my father followed behind with a teapot. I stayed beside Ellen on the sofa and my mother and father sat opposite us on two armchairs.

"It's a nice surprise to see you again Ellen after so long," said Mam. "We wondered what and where you were these days. How are your parents?"

"They're very well, Mrs Wilson, thank you," said Ellen, "these biscuits are delicious."

"John was delighted to be asked to your party weren't you son?" said Dad.

"Yes, very much so." I answered feeling my face had turned red for all to see. We chatted on about everything and had more tea. Suddenly, Mam said she needed to go to the shops and Dad said he'd give her a lift. I knew it was my mother's way of giving us time together alone. A spot of matchmaking, I reckoned.

"We hope to see more of you Ellen so do remember to come again soon," said Mam standing up to go.

"I will indeed Mrs Wilson, thank you. I'm going away for two weeks on Wednesday to Germany, but I will call again."

"Oh, John will miss you, won't you John?" I felt my face going red again and tried to smile.

"We better make a move." said Dad standing up and putting his good coat on. They left and we heard the door shutting behind them. I looked at Ellen and she looked back at me; we didn't say anything for a moment.

"Show me this document or explain what it is," I said.

"I can tell you what it is," she said. She took it in her hand and glancing over it she said,

"There was a young woman living in our house in my great, great grandfather's time. I've never heard this story before but it appears he met her in Eastern Europe while on his travels. They fell in love and he brought her to this country, to our house, his at the time. They were both young and got married quickly, somewhere in Moldova. This is a copy of the marriage certificate." she turned it over and there was a large bundle of pages stuck to the back of it with a large clip.

"What are those?" I asked pointing at the attached pages.

"They are my great, great grandfather's story. His parents died while he was young and he inherited the house, being an only child. He brought her back. She was called Ludmila. He brought back something else too." She stopped talking and I watched her go pale. I went to the kitchen and got her some water. When I returned, she was staring into space and her hands were shaking. I handed her the water and she quickly gulped it down.

"Oh John, how can I tell you this. Ludmila was never seen during the day. You see, she couldn't go out because she was a vampire."

Chapter 4

I stood with my mouth open; in shock. I couldn't believe what I was hearing. Ellen drank more water and looked long and hard at me.

"Say something for God's sake," she said still shaking. "Am I in danger of being attacked by some evil spirit?" I sat down and put my arm around her. She started to cry. I held her tighter and told her it would all be okay. I asked her about the document and what exactly it said.

"It's a kind of diary and letters all in one that my great, great grandfather kept. Surely, Dad knows about this as everything was passed to him since my great, great grandfather died. I've read some of it already. It's shocking, unbelievable. Does this explain what's happening in the house? I don't know if I can bring myself to read on. Will you read it with me?" she asked wiping her eyes with her handkerchief.

"Yes, I'll read it with you. My parents are not going to be here for a few hours so let me have a look." I opened the ancient document that she gave me and immediately I got a musty smell from the yellow pages. It felt dry and crinkly to touch. It was hard to make out in places, but I managed to read. It was titled:

My Encounter in Moldova
By Daniel Rackley 1838

Chisinau is a lovely city. I have been to Russia, Romania, and now Moldova. I have not kept a journal of my experiences in Russia or Romania, but I have in Moldova and for the following reason. Two weeks ago, I was on my way to a tavern. I had got to know some of the locals, though not very well. They were friendly enough but not intrusive. It was late evening and the darkness descended quickly. I felt the room in which I was staying, closing in on me and I longed for company. The family who I had engaged the house from were pleasant, but I didn't feel like talking with them that night. Having decided to go out, I locked the door behind me and set off carrying a lantern. As I walked through the woods that led from my lodgings to the inn, I thought of home. My parents now dead and I being the master of a large house. It made me sad to think of Mother and Father but at least they had left me well provided for. After I'd gone a short distance, I heard footsteps. They were soft but close behind me. I turned around and saw a beautiful young woman. She wore a blue cloak over a white dress. Her hair was dark in colour and I was struck by her paleness. She was carrying a small heavy stick in her hand. She stopped suddenly, as I turned, and I feared that she intended to rob me. Despite her beautiful face, I felt slightly afraid. Her mouth was firmly closed and her full red lips were clenched over her teeth. She stared at me and I stared back. Suddenly, I could see the tension or pent up rage or whatever it was passing from her. When I look back now it seems like we were standing like that for a long time but it would only have been seconds.

"I wasn't following you sir," she said. Her voice had a strange sound; I can't describe it.

"That's all right," I said.

"I didn't think you were…It's just that I didn't meet one person along the way and suddenly, there you were." She smiled and I couldn't be sure, but I thought I saw two sharp teeth, one on each side of her mouth. She quickly clenched her lips again. I found it difficult to turn and walk away, I knew I was staring, but I couldn't help it. Her gaze was almost hypnotic.

"Would you like to walk with me to the tavern?" I asked suddenly, coming back to my senses. "It's not far and you're welcome to join me. They have music there in the evenings, a kind of very small orchestra."

"I will go to the tavern with you, but I would like to sit outside in the moonlight listening to the music. I do not wish to go indoors, is this agreeable with you?" She had good English despite her strong Moldovan accent.

"Yes, of course," I said. We walked on by the light of the lantern. I suddenly began to feel colder. It was like a sudden drop in the temperature. It felt as though the icy feeling was coming from her.

We reached the tavern and there were tables outside with candles and white tablecloths placed on them. I could hear the music coming from inside. It sounded lovely in the still night. We sat down and I immediately tried to warm my hands from the candles. I had never experienced cold like it in my life. She watched me as I held my hands over the flames. Soon afterwards, the innkeeper came out. I noticed my strange companion looked downward, as I asked him for beer for myself and red wine in a tall glass as that was what she wanted. She sat a little far back from me and only her eyes and forehead were clearly visible in the candlelight. Her eyes though beautiful, had at the same time a look of ferocity in them.

"I like music," she said suddenly, turning her head away from me and looking into the darkness. "I used to listen to it a lot when I lived at home with my parents. They had musical

evenings sometimes. I would sit and listen to the musicians for hours. Piano and violin were my favourites. Sometimes, I fancy, I still hear the music; it follows me around, I suppose. Do you believe that's possible?"

"Anything is possible, when we love something," I replied feeling a bit surprised by the suddenness of her strange question. She gave a quick smile with her lips closed and then stared at the candles. I felt sadness coming from her as though she was thinking back on former happier days. I didn't want the mood to descend and I pointed out to her that the drinks were on the way as I saw the innkeeper carrying a tray and coming in our direction.

I paid him and he left without saying anything. I passed the dark red wine to my mysterious friend and lifted my glass, "To our meeting on this dark night." She raised her glass and touched it against mine. I noticed her nails were long. She brought the glass to her lips and again I caught a glimpse of the white sharp teeth. I put my glass down and lit a cigar.

"Permit me to introduce myself," I began, "I am Daniel Rackely and I live in Ireland. I will be in Moldova for a short time more and then I will go home again. My father died some months ago and I have inherited a large house with an estate. I have been travelling for quite a long time now and have been to Russia and Romania. I wanted to travel before settling down to running a large estate. My mother has been dead for several years. May I ask what your name is?" She hesitated and looked into my eyes with a look of longing. I can't put it any other way.

"I am Ludmila. I do not have any family here now. I would feel nothing if I left here. You've been very kind to talk to me and I thank you for the wine."

I felt I was being brought closer to her. It suddenly was feeling impossible for me to be not with her. I felt drawn to her but not in the usual way. It was as if she put a rope around my waist and pulled me to her. I found this woman who came out of the night, intriguing. There was a feeling of sadness about her but also a sense of mystery.

33

"Oh, I'm sorry to hear you don't have any family. Are they dead or living somewhere else?" I asked. I noticed she was running her tongue over her teeth under her closed lips.

"They are dead. When you have finished your drink would you like to walk in the woods and finish your cigar there?" she asked.

"That would be very nice," I answered.

"There is a full moon and a walk in the woods under its beams sounds delightful."

After about half an hour and some small talk we finished the drinks and lighting my lantern again, we walked back in the direction of the woods. She was walking closer to me now than she had been but didn't seem inclined to start a conversation. The trees looked black in the night and the light from the moon threw a grey shade on her face.

"Do you mind if we stop here for a moment?" she said suddenly, "My shoe has become loose."

"Not at all," I replied, "look there's a kind of homemade bench over there where we can sit down." We sat down on what seemed to be a seat of some description which looked like it had been carved from a fallen tree. She pulled up her dress slightly to get at her shoe. I turned my head in the opposite direction. Suddenly, I felt a coldness mixed with heat and turning around I saw that her mouth was slightly open with the sharp teeth close to my neck. Our eyes met and she suddenly stood up and said she had to hurry home. To me she looked like someone who was restraining herself.

"Is everything alright?" I asked. "You seem tense or frightened." She didn't answer me.

"May I see you again after tonight?" I asked. "Maybe tomorrow we could go into the city or have a picnic in the woods. It looks like it will be a nice day." She looked away from me towards the trees.

"Come," she said, "let us walk back together to the edge of the woods and we can say goodbye there." I picked up the lantern and put out my cigar. Suddenly, she put her arm in mine and we were linking. It was a nice feeling to have her

near me but that chill remained and nothing would make it go away.

"Is everything alright?" I asked stopping for a moment and looking at her.

"I am, but…" she said tightening her grip on my arm, "I'm glad I met you tonight. No!" she said noticing my face, "I'm not in any danger. Please don't worry about me."

We walked on and reached my lodging which was just beside the edge of the wood. To me it now looked terribly lonely, so still in the darkness. There was a coach outside with a driver sitting up on top. He wore a thick red scarf around his neck and a black top hat. He glared at me as I spoke with Ludmila. I could feel his resentment at me talking to her. I reckoned he was aged about sixty-five.

"I'd like to see you home safely," I said, "it's late and I don't know how far you have to go."

"There is no need. Dimitrie, here is my driver and protector. He will take me to where I live. It has been an interesting evening but now I must hasten away." She turned towards the coach and Dimitire jumped down and opened the door. It was padded inside with rich cushions. When she sat inside, Dimitire went to shut the door quickly. She stopped him with a wave of her hand. He left us and climbed back up into the driver's seat.

"Come inside for a moment," she said to me. "I feel there is something you want to ask me." I climbed in and immediately I felt the chill all around me. I saw her staring at me as I pulled the collar of my coat up higher.

"I do have something to ask you Ludmila. I would like to meet you again. I don't want to return home without knowing you better. I only just met you tonight and yet I feel a bond, perhaps even a loving bond." She smiled at me and then quickly stopped, remembering to not expose her sharp teeth too much.

"I once read somewhere that there are people who give their hearts quickly; perhaps you are one, Daniel, if I may call you that." I told her that I wished she would. She looked at me and then at the night sky. "I must be away before it gets *any later," she said. "I'm not available during the day, but I will send Dimitrie with a note of where we may meet again and you can give him a return note to me if you like. Does this suffice?"*

"Oh yes, indeed. Please don't forget me," I replied. I had fallen in love with this mysterious woman. She pulled on a pair of gloves and extended her hand to me.

"Goodnight Daniel, I won't forget you. You will hear from me soon, now that I know where you are living." I took her hand but this time it felt warm with the velvet glove.

"Goodbye!" I said stepping from the coach. "Soon."

"Goodbye," she answered, "you will hear from me in days." She put her hand to her forehead and then spoke loudly to her driver.

"Dimitrie, we must hurry, drive on." He cracked his whip and the coach was rattling down the road. I watched until it went out of sight. A short time later I found myself back inside my sitting room. I sat down and lit a cigar. I started to picture her face in the clouds of smoke that now drifted in front of me. Grey streaks were starting to appear in the sky by the time I retired. I didn't think I'd sleep that night and dreamt that Ludmila was in my room standing over me. I awoke but there was nobody there. I did however feel that same chill that I had felt earlier when I was with her. It was all around me and in the bed also. I imagined her face and grew restless thinking about when I might see her again. I hoped it would be soon.

Chapter 5

Ellen looked in disbelief as we read the strange journal. I didn't know what to think.

"There's more," she said. "I haven't read it all yet, but I want to read it with you. I have my car outside we could drive back to the cliff walk. There's that tearooms."

"Okay," I said, "let's go then. My parents will be back soon. I want to be able to finish reading this in peace without being asked questions about you." She looked pleasantly surprised.

"About me? I wonder why that is."

"Because", I replied, "they think you're very nice and they're right." She smiled and pinched my nose.

Half an hour later we found ourselves at the tearooms on the cliff walk. It had always been a favourite place of mine. It was just off the walk and in a sheltered spot. The couple who ran it, Paul and Jill were friendly, and knew us well. They had never seen us together there so I felt we were giving them something to talk about. The view of the sea was beautiful. It seemed very far down from where we were sitting. Sometimes it looked green and then blue. I ordered tea and two jam doughnuts and we sat in a corner under an old storm-lantern. There were pictures of ships and lighthouses around the walls. There was nobody else there at the time but us which added to our feeling of cosiness. Jill dropped down the tea and doughnuts. She told us to enjoy them and she smiled in a knowing kind of way at us both. We smiled back. I put the ancient papers on the table.

"It looks like there's still a lot more to read," I said flipping through the wrinkled dry dirty paper. Ellen took it from me and said it was her turn to read. She swallowed a bite from the doughnut, drank some tea and began to read.

It was two days later before I heard from Ludmila. I was driven mad wondering when I would get to meet her again. It happened on a windy afternoon. I was returning from a walk when I saw her coach outside the little house, in which I was staying. Dimitrie was sitting up on the driver seat looking as grim as ever. I walked toward him and he jumped down to meet me.

"I have a letter for you from Ludmila. She has told me to wait for your answer." I took it from him and opened it. It read:

Dear Daniel,

If you wish to meet with me again, I would be very happy to see you. I could call to you if that would suit. If you do wish to meet me, I will come to your lodging at 9 o' Clock tomorrow night. Please give Dimitrie a written reply if this is convenient for you. I cannot be there before 9 tomorrow night.

Ludmila.

"Wait here!" I said to the surly driver. I went into the house and grabbing pen and ink, I wrote the following note.

Dear Ludmila,

The time you give is convenient to me. I look forward to seeing and talking with you again.

Daniel.

I went back outside and handed the folded up note to Dimitrie. He snatched it from me and drove off sharply. I could feel my spirits rising at the thought of meeting her again and for the next hour I was restless in anticipation. I went to a museum later in the day to try and take my mind off the visit. I then had lunch with some of the locals I had gotten to know in the Inn. I wanted to tell them about Ludmila, but I kept control of my feelings. I stayed at home that night and sat out on the porch looking into space. Everything was so still around me and it felt almost eerie. In a short time more, I would be leaving Moldova and going home. Home to who? I asked myself. My parents were dead. I was now the owner of a large house and land but apart from the staff, I had nobody. I had friends but nobody close to me. Ludmila had no family either. I thought to myself maybe she would come with me. I knew it was outlandish; I'd only met her once. I made up my mind that I was not going without asking her to come with me. We could share our loneliness as well as our love. I retired to bed and again I felt that strange chill around me. It brought with it an empty longing unsettled feeling. I'd never felt anything like it before.

The following evening, I had red wine and cheese with some fruit and nuts prepared. I put a nice clean white table cloth with lighted candles on the table. Precisely at 9 o'clock I heard the coach pulling up outside. I opened the door and Dimitrie was helping Ludmila to alight. She looked even more radiant than when I'd seen her last. She smiled at me through her closed lips. I took her cold hand and led her to my door. She turned around and said to her driver,

"Come for me in two hours and now leave us." Dimitrie jumped back up on the seat and cracked his whip. The horses shot forward, leaving us alone. We went inside and I took her cloak. She wore a blue dress underneath with a black velvet band around her neck.

"You look lovely tonight, Ludmila," I said feeling in love with her. She smiled, again with her closed mouth and took my hand.

"You are very kind to me. I don't know if I deserve these compliments. Tell me more about why you have come here and of your home in Ireland, I want to know all about you." We sat down at the table and I poured the wine. I proceeded to tell her about my life and how I had wanted to travel before setting down. I told her about coming into my inheritance and my plan to run the estate. She brought the glass of wine to her lips and drank from it. I got a quick glimpse of the two sharp teeth of either side of her mouth. She saw this and tried to distract my attention by asking me about a picture on the wall. I told her I had no idea who it was as I was only a lodger and would be leaving soon.

Later we went for a walk around the edge of the woods. I felt happy to have her by my side. I had fallen in love. I wondered did she feel the same about me. We stopped and leaning against a tree, we kissed. There was nothing cold in the kiss.

"I love you," I said.

"Ah but you don't know much about me. I wonder if you would say that, if you knew everything." I told her I would and as we would get to know each other we would make our decisions based on that. This time she took me by surprise and kissed me on the neck. I could feel her sharp teeth through her lips. She quickly pulled back again and I sensed some unease or restraint in her. To me it seemed as though she was trying very hard to hold herself back.

"Can we go back to the cottage now?" she asked suddenly, with tears in her eyes.

"Yes, of course," I said taking her hand and walking back toward my little house. She was quiet and didn't seem inclined to talk. At the sight of the tears, I wanted to ask her if she felt well or if there was something the wrong, but I knew she didn't want me to refer to it. When we got inside, she looked at the clock and said Dimitrie would be here soon.

"Please sit-down Daniel," she said as if she was going to give me some bad news. I sat down and waited for her to speak. She walked over to the other side of the room and then walked back.

"You say you love me but you know very little about me."

"Please don't say anymore," I said, "except tell me that you will be my wife and come back to Ireland with me." She was quiet for what seemed like a long time.

"Dimitire will be here soon and I will leave with him. I will send him tomorrow with a letter from me explaining a lot of things. If after reading the letter you still want to bring me *to Ireland as your wife, then I will gladly go. First though you must think wisely." I felt my heart sink. Here was someone I was in love with at first sight and I just knew there was a problem. It wasn't going to stop me.*

"Come back to Ireland as my wife," I said.

"When you have read the letter, I want you to think carefully and then you can reply by letter to me through Dimitrie. I hear the coach coming." and she reached for her cloak. We walked out in to the night air. The coach pulled up and after getting in to it, Ludmila told me to except her letter tomorrow night.

"Goodnight my love!" she said leaning forward and kissing me through the open coach window. I kissed her back.

"Goodnight Ludmila," I whispered, "I can't wait to get your letter and to show you how we can move forward." She smiled and put her hand on my cheek.

"Soon," she said, "hopefully very soon. Drive on Dimitrie." The crack of the whip was heard and they were both gone into the night leaving me with a muddled head.

Chapter 6

"Well!" said Ellen as she stopped reading. "What do you think?"

"It's very unusual or strange or something, I don't know what I'd call it." I answered feeling perplexed.

"There's still quite a bit to read. We're not going to get it done today. Do you have any plans for this evening?" I asked.

"No, I'm free, I think. I'm going into town with my sisters on Sunday morning. You remember meeting them at the party don't you, Mary and Caroline?"

"Yes,"

"Okay I'll meet you at three o' clock at the gate to the park. We can get something to eat if you like, and continue our read." She looked at me for a second without saying a word. Suddenly, I felt that I'd over stepped the mark but then she must have seen my face.

"It's alright," she said, "I'd like that. So, three o' clock then. I'll bring the motor car." We got up to leave.

"I'll drop you off," she said, "it's not far." I said, "Okay!" and we headed out to the car. We got in and drove towards my house. I still had the diary in my hand so I stuffed it into Ellen's bag. She smiled but didn't say anything. We drove along in silence; thinking about what we'd read, I suppose, and finding it hard to believe. Suddenly, Ellen broke the silence.

"Would you fancy another cup of tea, this time in my house?" I was delighted to be asked.

"Yes," I replied, "that would be lovely. Will your parents be there or any of your family?"

"Yes, some of them I suppose but don't worry we can sit in the gazebo and have tea brought out to us; you'd like that wouldn't you?" I smiled, that was answer enough for her. The thought of sitting drinking tea in a gazebo with Ellen Rackley was very nice.

We arrived at the entrance to the house. We passed through tall iron gates with pillars on each side. On top of each pillar was a large granite ball. She drove the car on further and a little to the left of the house. We stopped and got out. Dillon, the butler, came towards us.

"Hello Dillon, can you arrange for us to get tea and biscuits in the gazebo?"

"Certainly, my lady, I'll see to it right away." He left us and I followed her through the long grass towards the ornate structure.

"I prefer to walk through the grass rather than use the path," she said, "except of course if it's raining and the grass is wet, but then of course I wouldn't be sitting out here in the rain." We sat down on two white chairs. A maid came out with the tea and a plate filled with a selection of biscuits. It was a funny feeling, sitting there, drinking tea and eating biscuits with the noise of the crows cawing in the tall trees.

"Are you ready to hear more," she asked.

"I'll give you a break," I said, "I'll read this time." she handed me the wrinkled paper.

My Encounter in Moldova
Continued
Daniel Rackley 1838

The next part of this diary is going to be hard to believe. If anyone should ever get to read it, let me assure them it's a true account. I got up early the following morning and went for some breakfast. The people who owned the house had prepared nice food. After breakfast, I went and stood at the open front door but there was no sign of Dimitrie. I walked to the tavern for tobacco and as I walked back through the woods, I thought of my first meeting with Ludmila. It seemed like an age ago but in reality it was no time at all. So, I thought to myself what does the future hold? I was now a wealthy man with property and a fine house. Would Ludmila marry me and then leave Moldova to live in Ireland? She would have a good life with me and not want for anything. In a short time more, I would be leaving Moldova. I would have to leave but not without Ludmila, I hoped.

I reached my house and went inside. I sat down and tried to read, but I was too restless. I could find no peace and grew impatient. I lay on the sofa and must have dozed off. I woke up feeling cold, to the sound of carriage wheels crunching on the gravel at the front of the house. I went to the hall door and opened it. Dimitrie was sitting on the driving seat of the coach looking very proud and defiant. I went outside and asked if he'd brought something for me. He handed me what looked like a long letter of some sort. I took it from him. It was sealed with red wax.

"My orders," he said, "are to come back in the afternoon between three and four o' clock for your reply. Only one word

is required from you, yes or no." I nodded to him and suddenly, he cracked the whip and the horses dashed forward, leaving me in a cloud of dust. I felt the letter in my hand and saw a coat of arms on the wax seal. I went inside, got myself some tea and sat down to read what she had written. When I'd broken the seal there seemed to rush at me a heavy smell of dust or something ancient. I couldn't account for it, as the paper on which it was written looked new. I folded it back and read:

Ludmila's story

Dear Daniel,

I have sat down and prepared this letter for you to read and decide what will be your next course of action. I don't intend to sway you in any direction. When you've read it you will understand.

I was part of a noble family here in Moldova. I'm not going to say where exactly or who the family were, but my life was good and I didn't want for anything. My parents were kind to us all; I had brothers and sisters.

One night, I went with some friends to an old deserted church. We had heard old tales of seeing ghosts at twelve o' clock if one went and sat under an old tree, there in the small graveyard. I decided to go with my two friends to see if we would see anything. I was approaching nineteen years of age at the time and enjoying life. There was somebody who I was interested in but nothing had yet blossomed. Perhaps it would have if things had gone differently for me, but they didn't. I remember, it was a calm night and there was a full moon. We waited impatiently under the tree but nothing appeared to us. We decided to go home after an hour or so but as we were leaving through the old iron gate a man in black approached us. He startled us as he came upon us suddenly.

"Please don't be alarmed," he said noticing our shocked faces. He didn't say anything else but just stood looking at us. We asked him what he was doing there at that time of night. He told us that he couldn't sleep and he found the quiet night

air and a walk the best thing to help him find sleep. He had a handsome face with a thick blonde moustache. His head was covered by a wide black hat. He spoke Moldovan and carried a lantern in his hand. He asked us what we were doing there and we told him. He laughed at the idea of us wanting to see a ghost. We told him we had to leave and he insisted on escorting us. We were glad because we had to cross some dark fields and pass through a narrow lane on the way back. I found myself heavily attracted to this man. He spoke little as we all walked along, but I could feel him in my head. I was falling under his influence. I liked it.

I lived a little further on from the others and after saying goodbye, I walked on with the handsome stranger walking beside me. I tried to observe him more closely as he walked. I thought there was a sadness about him mixed with adventure and at the same time something unpleasant. I couldn't put my finger on it. He looked at me now and again as we walked and I just knew he could read my thoughts.

"My house is here," I said suddenly, arriving at the familiar gates to my home. I had been so distracted by his looks that I hardly noticed the long walk. "Thank you for escorting me home." He bowed and took off his hat, revealing his lustrous blonde hair.

"Goodbye!" he said in a deep voice, "I hope you sleep well." Suddenly, he was gone; it was as though he just vanished. I couldn't remember him walking away. I wondered if I'd gone blank, as there seemed to be no other explanation for it. I went straight to my room and prepared for bed. My parents were still up reading, sometimes they liked to go to bed late. I went back downstairs and went inside to where they were sitting.

"Ah you're home," said my mother, "did you have a nice walk with your friends?" I told her I did and that we enjoyed ourselves. I didn't say anything about the stranger in black.

"Goodnight dear!" she said. "It's late and we'll see you in the morning." My father smiled and nodded over to me. I climbed the stairs with a strange feeling of excitement coming over me. It felt like a forbidden excitement. I liked the air of

46

mystery about the stranger in the graveyard. I reached the bedroom, lit a candle, and got ready for bed. I put the candle out and was asleep in no time, despite my excitement. I fell into a deep sleep and had the strangest dreams. I dreamt the stranger in black was in my room and that he leaned over me and bit me on the neck. I soon realised it wasn't a dream but yet I felt powerless. I didn't feel pain but instead a strange wild pleasure. I seemed to drift off into clouds. I was happy to go, such was the feeling of ecstasy.

The next day, when I awoke, I was not at home. I was in some dark castle with high arched ceilings. I wasn't me anymore. I never got to see my family or friends again because I had gone beyond them. When I felt that bite on my neck, I left all that I knew. This happened a long, long time ago. I can't die in the normal way and so I live on. I am a vampire, one of the undead. My master who brought me to this way of life was sought out and staked through the heart, one of the ways to kill a vampire. I fled with two others at the time. I lost them somehow and after days of sleeping and nights of prowling, I met Dimitrie. He was a man alone; a lost soul, I suppose, you could call him and he accepted what I was. He had quite a lot of knowledge about vampires. He took me to his small house and has looked after me ever since. He was lonely and it made him feel happy to know there was someone there when the nights were cold and friendless. He protects me and obtains what I need in the way of food. I will not go into details on that. I have lived with him for a good number of years now. I have not felt any desire for love or physical contact since becoming a vampire and thought it was now gone from me. That was until I met you. Ever since that night when I met you in the woods, I have felt differently. I admit, I may have entertained other intentions when I followed you that night, but when you looked at me; I became disarmed.

So, Daniel, this is it. My family are all long dead now as many years have passed. I will go with you to your country, as your wife if you like. It would be a strange marriage would it not? Dimitrie will be back tomorrow and you must give him a one-word answer, yes if you would like me to come with you, or a no and we say goodbye for ever. I do have a curse on me, but I would love you like no other could.

Until I hear from you again,
Ludmila.

I folded the letter and put it in my pocket. My mind was thrown into a mixture of shock, confusion, and anger. I was angry that this person I had fallen deeply in love with was a creature of the night, not a real person anymore. The whole thing appalled me. That was my head speaking, but my heart said something else. It told me that Ludmila was the one that I wanted and I would not rest until I had her with me for all time. I left the house and went for a walk through the woods. I thought of our first meeting as I walked. I arrived at the tavern and ordered a drink. I took her letter from my pocket and read it again. I thought of the future with her and without her. I could feel the innkeeper looking at me, as I read the letter over and over. I left after an hour and returned home. I spent the next few hours in agony, I tried to imagine myself leaving Moldova alone and arriving back home with a new life opening for me. The scene was pleasant in my mind, but it wouldn't have Ludmila in it and that I wasn't prepared to accept. I then thought about how we could carry it off when we returned to my house. It all seemed so absurd and I couldn't imagine what it meant for the future. How would I explain her not being available to come outside with me during the day?

After much agonising and pacing the room, I decided to take her with me. I wasn't sure how I intended to do this, but she would be coming back with me. I went to bed very late that night and slept little, wondering what my next step would be and was I doing right. Such is the way of love and as I said before, we plunge in or we don't.

Chapter 7

"Stop for a minute please." Ellen sounded upset. "I can't take this. What or where is it leading to? I want to get out of that house. How can I stay there with that woman or whatever it is, wandering the corridors?" I took her hand in mine.

"What do you want me to do?" I asked.

"Read on, we have to…I hate it all."

"Okay, if you're sure." I picked up the old yellowing paper and started to read again.

I woke next morning with the sunlight in the room. I had not pulled the blind down all the way the night before and the light managed to get in. I got up and washed my face. I spotted the letter on the chair where I'd thrown it the night before. It all came back to me with a crash. Today was the day that her faithful driver would be coming back and I must have an answer for her. I had a light breakfast and sat drinking tea, wondering when Dimitrie would arrive.

I walked up and down the room, tossing it over in my mind. Finally, I sat down and wrote a short note saying one word, Yes. I folded it over and sealed it. My hands were shaking.

After about an hour I heard the rattle of wheels and I walked out to the porch. I could see Dimitrie's grim face staring at me as the horse approached the door. The coach drew up beside me and he put his hand out.

"Ludmila awaits your reply," he said.

"Here it is, take care not to lose it." He snatched it from my hand. He cracked his whip and the horses moved forward leaving me wondering what had I done. Well, I thought to

myself, it's done now for better or for worse, but I love Ludmila and that is what's important for me. I went straight to the inn and ordered a brandy. I couldn't stop shaking.

"Are you alright my friend?" asked the innkeeper, "You don't look too good."

"I'm fine please, there's no need to worry. May I have some bread and coffee too?" He brought them and in my state of nervousness or whatever it was, I devoured them rapidly.

I didn't hear from Ludmila until later. Well into the evening when the sun had gone, there was a knock on the door. I hadn't heard the carriage wheels. On opening the door, I saw her standing outside. She smiled with her mouth shut. I told her to come in and she walked to the sofa and sat down. Her feet made no sound. I sat beside her and we were both silent. Suddenly, her gentle voice broke the silence.

"So, Daniel, I got your message and it made me very happy. I know, how you feel about me and I about you. Now that you know the spell that is on me, do you really want to marry me and take me to your country?"

"Yes!" I said and I hugged her. It seemed I was prepared to overlook this awful thing that had happened to her. I was taking her into my life. Did I really know what I was doing? I asked myself. Could I know happiness for the future? I felt certain I would not know it if I let her go.

"You are perhaps still not sure am I right?" she asked.

"No!" I replied. "I am sure. I just don't know how this will work out. There will be people to meet and life must go on as normal. I am wondering how to bring this off."

"Have you come up with anything?" she asked.

"Yes, I have. I am known to one of the town officials here and he has the power to celebrate at a civil marriage. I know if I ask him, he will marry us any time we want to. It can be in the evening when it's dark."

"Once it's not in a church, you must see that. If it is to happen, can we do it here in this room with just the two of us and Dimitri as a witness?" The question of Dimitri had been going around in my mind for some time. Where did he fit in to our plan? I didn't want to bring him to Ireland. I wanted him out of Ludmila's life; our lives.

"Let me speak with the official tomorrow," I said. She stood up and asked me when it would be.

"Friday would be a good day or evening should I say. There is a ship sailing that night and it will take some time to get to Scotland and then to Cork in Ireland. I live in the western part of the county. You'll like it there."

"I will like it anywhere once I am with you," she replied. I felt my love for her growing stronger, but I couldn't help thinking about how we'd carry it off.

"Today is Tuesday," she said, "I will come here on Friday evening at nine o' clock. Have this official friend of yours ready to marry us at half nine."

"This is my plan," I said. "We will be married. I will pay him and he'll be gone. You have Dimitrie outside with your clothes packed and I will give him my case. We will then leave for the port. It will still be dark when we get there. You can stay in the cabin with the blind drawn during the day. When we arrive, it will be night and my house is a short journey so it will still be dark when we get there. Soon, we will be gone from here." She walked from me and looked at the floor in a reflective kind of way. I said nothing but watched to see what she would do next. Suddenly, she turned around and looked hard at me.

"Do you really believe this can work?" she asked. I told her I did. She said that I must be mad to want to marry a vampire, a creature of the night. She said she was sure about wanting to marry me but asked, was I?

"Yes," I said. "I want to marry you."

"What about Dimitrie? He's been with me for a good long time now and it will hurt him when I say goodbye. He knows my needs and he will be very jealous of you taking his place."

"I'm not just taking his place; I am becoming your husband," I said feeling a bit annoyed. She took my hand in hers and I felt its coolness.

"Don't let our first disagreement be over the ever faithful Dimitrie. I will talk to him; he should feel happy for me now that I've found love. You still haven't answered my question."

"What is it?" I asked.

"Do you really believe this can work?" I told her I did.

"I have a question to ask you Ludmila," I said.

"Oh and what is that?" she replied looking a bit surprised.

"I know what vampires need and I wondered what you intended to do when we reach Ireland." She looked hard at me.

"Ah," she answered, "you do have concerns. Are you afraid that one night I will not be able to control my bloodlust and attack you? Do you fear I will contaminate you and that you will become one of the undead?" I felt terrible but these indeed were my concerns. I even wondered how Ludmila was surviving now and who or what were her victims. She gave a small clenched smile.

"I can see by your eyes that you do have fears," she said. "Let me put your mind at ease. When my master had control over me, yes, I did have victims. When he was killed off, I did not have the desire to attack human beings anymore. I attacked sheep when the need arose. When I met Dimitrie, he understood a lot about the curse that was on me. He had experience in this area. He produced for me a solution containing blood and sugar. It is not human blood. This has kept me alive, kept me alive so that I would meet you one day. If Dimitrie is not coming with us, we must get his directions on how to make this concoction." She stood up suddenly, "I must leave now. Until Friday, my love." We hugged and I did indeed love her and had no doubt she loved me. It was just the whole business seemed so bizarre. She went to the door. The carriage wasn't outside and I offered to walk with her.

"No, it's alright, I see Dimitri standing outside. One of the shafts needed repair and so he walked me over." I could see the grim face of Dimitri looking at her and then at me. She went to him and they disappeared amongst the dark trees. I went back inside and wrote a quick note to the official

informing him of what I wanted him to do and when. The next morning, I gave it to the son of the couple who owned the house in which I was staying. I told him to wait for an answer. I went for a walk in the woods and then returned to sit on the porch. I waited anxiously for his reply and tried to imagine what it would be. I didn't have to wait long. Within an hour the young boy came back with the note. I saw him making his way from the woods to my porch. He came running and handed me a sealed note.

"Thank you!" I said giving him a few coins for his trouble.

"Thank you, sir, thank you very much." I went inside and closed the door and quickly opened the note, it read.

Dear Daniel,

I got your note and it's nice to hear from you again. Yes, I can marry you on Friday in the evening, but it's highly unusual at such short notice. When or where did you meet this woman? You are indeed a dark horse. You can count on me to come. I'll be there at half past eight. I hope to raise a glass to you and your new wife.

Vadim Carman.

I crunched up the piece of paper in my hand. It's done now, I thought to myself, I'm marrying a vampire.

Chapter 8
The Diary Continued

It didn't take long for Friday to come around. I had our tickets and my case was packed on Thursday night. I asked the old couple who owned the cottage that I was staying in, to come to the wedding. I also asked their son. It would be nice, I thought, to have some sort of gathering, but I also felt terrible. It felt like I was deceiving everyone. I had fallen in love with Ludmila and anybody who saw and met her could understand why but if only they knew the truth. I spent the night pacing up and down the room. I went out for a walk in the woods. I always walked there when I had things on my mind. The night was the darkest I'd seen in a while and the woods seemed like one black shape around me. I lit a cigar and listened to a bird of some sort making a screeching noise in the still black night. I sat there for about an hour, pondering everything and asking myself the same question over and over, what is love. Is this love, I asked myself, when I am prepared to overlook my future life living with a vampire. Didn't Ludmilla deserve happiness after what had happened to her? Everything went around in my mind until I became weary and retired for the night.

The next morning, I was up about nine o' clock and got breakfast delivered from my landlord. He said his wife wanted to give me a treat on such a special day. I thanked him and told him I looked forward to seeing him and his family at the wedding at 9 p.m.

"Nothing would give me more pleasure. We don't often have special occasions here, so it's some excitement for us."

"I don't mean to disappoint you Alexandru," I said, "but it will be a very simple ceremony."

"A chance for us to wear something nice." He left and I shut the door behind him. The sun was shining through the lace curtains, but it was still cold outside. I sat down and enjoyed the food. I remember thinking about how this was my last breakfast as a single man.

Vadim arrived in the evening at eight o' clock. He was dressed in a black suit and looked very official. He carried a black hard covered book under his arm. Despite his grave exterior, he was pleasant and polite. He shook my hand and I noticed how firm his grip was.

"Ah, Daniel, my friend, a big day for you. Why did you keep it so quiet? You're a dark horse, never mind, that's your affair. I can give you the certificate immediately." I was starting to get anxious and couldn't wait for Ludmila to arrive. I could see my life passing before my eyes. I felt the strangest feelings rising in me. I couldn't put the feelings into words. They were not feelings of doubt, I loved Ludmila, but I wondered who else would marry a vampire. I wanted her, but I wanted the blight to leave us.

At twenty minutes to nine, I heard the carriage. I went outside and Ludmila was alighting, she looked beautiful in white with a cream shawl over her shoulders. She was wearing a white bonnet with a yellow ribbon on it.

"Stop!" Ellen shouted and put her hand on the ancient pages.

"What is it?" I asked. She told me it was a woman in a white bonnet with a yellow ribbon that she'd seen at the window of her house when I arrived for the party.

"She was obviously brought here by my great, great grandfather. She's still here in some form and now she's walking amongst us. Why has nobody ever mentioned this? Did my parents never feel anything in the house?" I put my arm around her and asked her not to be upset, that somehow, we'd get to the bottom of it. She didn't look convinced and neither was I. How could anyone get their head around this?

Dillon arrived with fresh tea and we settled down to reading more of Daniel's story.

"Do you want to continue?" she asked.

"Maybe for a little bit more," I replied. "It's just such a strange story." I picked up the diary and began to read again.

Ludmila seemed anxious for the ceremony. I quickly introduced her to the family who I'd been staying with and to Vadim. I noticed none of them smiled very much when they shook her hand. I was glad, she had it in a glove or they might have shuddered at the cold feel. They seemed to hold back from her. It wasn't very reassuring on our wedding day. Vadim quickly arranged our seating. I sat facing him with Ludmila by my side. Dimitri sat behind us and behind him were Alexandru and his family. It was all very official and legal and the deed was soon done. Dimitri acted as a witness, signing his name just below ours. After the ceremony, Alexandru's wife brought in a cake and I made some tea and opened a bottle of wine. Most of us had tea but Ludmila wanted the red wine. I watched as she carefully drank from the long-stemmed glass trying not to show her two fangs like teeth. I noticed Ludmila's surname was Rosca and Dimitri's was Lisnic. I thanked the Bivol family (Alexandru, his wife Veronyka and son Andrei for their kindness to me during my stay in Moldova).

"Think nothing of it my friend," said Alexandru, "we loved having you and will miss you when you return home. The journey will not be so lonely now that you have a beautiful wife to sail with you." He tried to smile and quickly called a toast to the new married couple. We all raised our glasses except Veronyka. She was staring at Ludmila from behind. I thought this very odd behaviour. She switched her eyes in my direction and beckoned with them for me to approach her. I put down my glass and went over to her. She looked hard at me and asked me what I was doing. I told her I was getting married and what did she think I was doing.

"You know what I'm talking about," she said sharply. "This Ludmila is not like other women. I have seen her on two

occasions in the woods at night wandering around in freezing cold, dressed only in a nightdress. Her teeth are jagged also. It all points to one thing. She might have everybody fooled but not me. I know about these things."

"Stop, stop it now," I said quietly. "This is my wedding day and I am not going to listen to any nonsense. Your family have been kind to me during my stay here and I am very grateful, but I am leaving tonight. Let me leave on a pleasant note."

"Very good, if this is truly what you want, I can only wish you good luck; you'll need lots of it." She walked quickly away to her husband.

After about an hour they all left except for Dimitri.

"Wait outside for a moment." she told him and her faithful protector went outside and sat on the carriage. Ludmila hugged and kissed me hard as if it was to be her last kiss. There were tears in her eyes.

"Not sad today surely," I said.

"I am crying because I am happier than I have been in a long time. I hope you will be happy too." I told her I was sure, I would.

"There is one more thing," she said. I noticed how she was no longer trying to hide the sharp teeth from me.

"What is it?" I asked.

"I need Dimitri. He knows what I need to survive. Only he knows. He will follow us on in a few days. Is this alright with you?" I told her I was a bit disturbed by this and I did not bank on bringing him back.

"You can tell them at your house that I have some mystery illness and that he is a healer who can look after me. They will accept this. You can say that. You don't want him around the place, but he is vital to my health."

"I have a small cottage on the estate and it's empty now. He can stay there. I don't want him living in my house," I said.

"I do not have a problem with that and neither will he." We kissed again.

"Let me get my case and you tell Dimitri what we have agreed." She put her shawl over her shoulders again and went outside. I got the case and the tickets and took a last look at the small house where I'd been staying. I blew the candles out and stepped outside. Ludmila was already in the coach and Dimitri was looking his usual grave self, sitting on the driver's seat. He jumped down and took my luggage from me. He then opened the door of the coach and I got in beside my new wife. My loneliness was gone in an instant. I had a new wife and I was heading to a new life. I didn't know what that life would be like. I was aware of the strange circumstances of my marriage, but I felt loved and I in turn loved my bride. We heard the whip cracking and the coach jerked forward. I felt Ludmila's gloved hand on my arm.

"What an adventure," I said. She smiled and said she couldn't ever remember being this happy.

"We are not having a honeymoon, but it will take some time for us to reach Cork and then a journey by coach to my house. My parents are dead, I have no family, but I have a lot of staff at my house and when you meet them, they will love you too."

"I hope so," she said, "I do so much want to be loved by everyone that I meet. My life with the master left me thinking that I would never ever again know real love. It was not my fault that this curse came upon me." Tears were starting to form in her eyes. I kissed her and told her there would be no more tears. She put her head on my shoulder. It had started to rain and as I watched the drops running down the windows of the coach, I wondered about the future.

Chapter 9

The evening was coming on and I told Ellen I had to go. She took the diary from me and put it under a small white table.

"Are you in work on Monday?" she asked.

"Yes, I start at nine." She looked in the direction of the house.

"So, is this Ludmila really in the house?" she asked.

"The next part of that mouldy old diary is going to tell us if she came here with my great, great grandfather. I don't think I can read on." She rose and stood with her back to me. I walked over to her and told her not to be frightened but that we needed to read the rest of the diary.

"We'll approach your parents or brothers and sisters, surely they know something."

"Can you imagine," she said laughing. "They think I'm half mad already. No, I want to rid my home of this Ludmila once and for all. I am going to postpone my trip to Germany. I couldn't relax with all this in the background. Will you help me in this?"

"Yes, of course I will. We don't know for definite if she is here, but then again who was that face at the window? I think I should be going home now. Give me a ring if anything should happen, or just ring me anyway if you want to." She looked up and smiled at me.

"Okay, I'll give you a lift."

On the way back, we were both very quiet, I suppose, we didn't know what to say. It was a strange tale but what did it mean for the future? I pitied Ellen living in that lovely big house but with something eerie walking its corridors at night or perhaps walking through walls. I'd read about vampires before, but I thought they were just folklore.

We arrived at my house and as I got out of the car, I thought, *Ellen looked a bit down.*

"I wish you were staying at my place tonight," she said sadly. I told her to call me any time of the day or night if she needed to. We kissed and I got out. She drove off and I watched as the car drove out of sight. I started to walk in the direction of my house and saw my mother looking out through the window. She withdrew quickly and came to the hall door as I got nearer. It felt good to see her. There was such an air of normality about her after all the stuff I'd been reading.

"Well," she said, "did they give you anything to eat?" I told her I had tea.

"Can I ask you something?" I asked. She looked at me puzzlingly.

"What is it?" she asked.

"Has there ever been any strange stories about the Rackley home?" She now looked at me as if I had two heads.

"Not that I know of but you could ask your father, he came from around here. What makes you ask?"

"Let's just say that Ellen is feeling something strange in the house and to be perfectly honest I did too when I was there at the party." Mam looked shocked, "I thought you enjoyed yourself."

"I did, I did but there is something eerie in that house," I said.

"All big houses have a name for having ghosts etc. That's all it is, nonsense, but ask your father, he's in the sitting room." I went in and found him sitting by the fire reading a book with a red cover. I thought he looked pale. I sat in the chair opposite him. He put down the book and smiled at me. "You look like you have something on your mind," he said with a knowing look. I asked him if he'd ever heard anything strange about the Rackley house. He stood up, walked to the window and stared out at the flowers. He turned in my direction and said that stories get passed down and yes, he'd heard of strange goings on in the house years ago, before his time.

"What sort of strange things?" I asked.

"I don't know much but there was a story of a strange woman who came to live there and then left. Local people were suspicious of her. She wasn't there for long, but it has been said that they were a bit afraid of her. Where is this coming from? Don't tell me you're going to let some old story frighten you away from Ellen Rackley."

"Sit down Dad, I want to tell you something." He walked back to the armchair and sat down again. I told him everything that had happened from the night of the party up until now. The look on his face went through many changes as he listened.

"Where is this diary now?" he asked. I told him Ellen had it.

"I'm sorry son but common sense prevents me from believing this story." I was annoyed with him.

"What about the diary?"

"Concentrate on Ellen not her ancestors, that's my advice to you. This thing, whatever you think it is, is not real. So, you found an old diary. Maybe this was put there for you or her to find. Ellen's great, great grandfather was probably a bit of a character and maybe he was having a laugh. Lighten up and get her to lighten up as well." I left him reading in the sitting room and went outside for a walk. I walked as far as the old mill and stood looking into the dark water, I liked to do that when I had things on my mind. I imagined Ellen sitting in the gazebo or her room all alone. I walked around the fields and then headed home again. Just as I got in, I heard the phone ringing. I answered it and Ellen was at the other end of the line.

"I hope I'm not disturbing you," she said.

"No, not at all. Are you alright?"

"I want to read some more of the diary, but I want you there too. Can you come over for an hour? There's nobody here until later. Maybe we could finish it. I can come and collect you in my motor."

"I'll be ready and waiting at the door. See you soon." She hung up and I proceeded to put my coat on and comb my hair.

"Oh!" said my mother as she passed by, "Have you got a date with a certain somebody?" I told her Ellen was coming around and that we were going for a drive in her car.

"That'll be nice. Be careful in that car and don't let Ellen drive too fast." A short time later I heard the engine outside. I rushed down the garden path. She smiled at me with that lovely smile of hers as I got in.

"Are you ready for more of this diary?" she asked.

"If you are, I am." and we drove off in the direction of her house. She was quiet for a minute and then suddenly, sprang into talking quickly.

"Today is ideal for reading more of the diary," she began, "they've all gone to town and won't be back until late. Dillon will be there, but he won't bother us. He's going to leave some chicken on a tray for us in the drawing room. I hope you like chicken." She turned and smiled at me when she said this.

"I love it," I replied, "I look forward to sitting in the drawing room and eating chicken with Ellen Rackley." I looked out the window at the rolling countryside and it was beautiful. As the trees whisked by, I found myself thinking of everything. It was as if my whole life was passing before my eyes. *Where was it all taking me,* I wondered.

Chapter 10

We arrived and parked the car at the front of the house. As I got out, I found myself glancing up at the windows; there was no face this time. I followed Ellen through the now familiar arched hallway, making our way to the drawing room. The house was silent and It felt strange being there. I suddenly started to feel apprehensive. I had been looking forward to just the two of us being here together but now there was a heaviness about the place. Ellen looked back at me and smiled. I smiled back, not wanting her to feel my nervousness. I so wanted her to be at ease and besides she had to live here.

We arrive at the drawing room's door and went in. There was a tray with a large teapot, chicken, and biscuits on it. I felt hungry and we both sat down and tucked in with zest.

"This would be so cosy," said Ellen, "if it wasn't for faces at windows and strange diaries."

"Is the diary here?" I asked. She put down her cup and walked over to a cabinet and opening the middle drawer she took out a kind of leather case. She opened it and the diary appeared again.

"Do you want to read while I finish my tea?" she asked. I took it from her hands and moved to the high-backed sofa in front of the fire. There was a knock on the door and Dillon came in.

"Was everything to your satisfaction, my lady?" he asked.

"Yes, thank you Dillon. I'll call you if I need anything."

"Very good, my lady." he left and shut the door behind him. I picked up the diary. It felt dirty and dry to touch with a kind of vinegar type smell coming from it. "Shall I begin?" I asked.

"Yes." was her definite reply. I began to read.

Daniel Rackley's journal continued

I am sitting here in my armchair by a nice fire writing this. I am, only now, getting a chance to continue my strange diary. Ludmila has just retired for the night. Dimitri is living in a cottage on the estate. I have given him employment and he seems content. He can be very sullen and resentful but perhaps I just need to get used to his ways. He supplies Ludmila with a strange mixture and only he knows the recipe. I must find out what it is and how it's arrived at. More than one person should know this. Our voyage went well and we have been here for a few months now. The staff seemed a bit suspicious of Ludmila at first, but I explained to Mrs Kirwan, the housekeeper, that my new wife had a rare condition which forces her to live in an unconventional manner. She seemed to accept this and passed it on to the other staff. It is indeed a strange existence, but I am happy and I think Ludmila is too. Sometimes she seems restless. I don't know if it's homesickness or a longing for her old life. When she is like this, we take walks in the dark. Sometimes, I feel the old way of life is calling her back. I am sure it's only Dimitri's mixture that prevents her from doing so. The staff seem to have accepted only seeing her after dark, though I'm sure they think it odd. For now, everything is alright, and I intend to close this diary unless something major happens in our lives.

Daniel Rackley 1838.

"That's not the end, surely!" said Ellen looking disappointed.

"There's more. Shall I read on?"

"Yes, of course. I just know there has to be an explanation or some hint, as to why there is something wrong in this house." I thought she sounded frustrated. I threw the words of Daniel Rackley on a table. "Who cares!" I said feeling fed up with it all. "What difference does it make to you or me here and now. I like you and I think you like me. This thing, whatever it is, will fade away." She walked over to the table and picked up the ancient papers. "Read on, this is my family we're talking about and I have a right to an answer." I could see she was getting hot under the collar. I smiled and took the diary from her. I could tell from the thickness that it was coming to an end. I sat down beside Ellen and began to read.

Daniel Rackley's journal continued

It is now 1841 and I have decided to resume the diary, as a lot of things have happened. Not long after my last entry, Dimitri died suddenly. The doctor said it was a heart attack. One of the men working on the estate found him in his cottage. He said there was a look of terror on his face. It was as if he's seen something terrible before he died. It was a dreadful shock but an even bigger one for Ludmila. She always spoke highly of Dimitri and what he was doing for her and how he had taken care of her in Moldova. I found it hard to console her. She became distant and I thought I saw a lot of fury in her eyes. There was another shock to come.

Two days later, the funeral took place. Ludmila could not attend, as it was during daylight hours. The staff of the house were all present and I'm sure they thought it strange that my wife should not be there. He was laid in a nice spot beside a tree. I always felt he resented me but now as the coffin was lowered into its last resting place, I felt his loss. I knew it was him who was keeping Ludmila on the straight and narrow. I was too of course loving her, as I did as her husband. He knew what she was capable of and he saved her from the reach of darkness.

Back home that night, the house was very quiet. I expected to see Ludmilla as usual in the drawing room, but she didn't come. I went straight to our bedroom. I found her sitting in the darkened room. She reached out to me and I sat beside her and took her hand; it was colder than usual. She said that she felt cut off from her own country following the death of Dimitri. She worried about the mixture. I told her to rest and not to think of all that for the moment. She smiled at me and I couldn't tell if I was imagining things, but her two teeth seemed longer and sharper. She saw me looking and the smile passed away quickly.

"You need to get some rest too," she said, "it's been a long day."

"Yes, you're right, why don't we both just lie on the bed for an hour or two." We lay down together and wrapping our arms around each other, we fell asleep almost immediately.

I woke about two hours later and Ludmila was not beside me. It had got darker since I'd fallen asleep and the room was cold. I lit the lamp and saw a folded sheet of paper on the pillow. It was addressed to me. As I opened it, I had the most horrible feeling of something wrong. It read as follows:

Dear Daniel,

I am gone from here and from you. Because I am a vampire, I have powers and can return to my native country without difficulty. You and your household are in danger from me. Someone, from my past found out about me and came to Dimitri. I believe, he caused his death. I don't have very much of Dimitri's substitute so I must seek real blood soon. If I stayed here, I would sooner or later contaminate you. In short, I would either kill you slowly or worse again, you would become one of the undead. I would end up falling under the curse of this person; from my past. He is evil and you are not safe as long as I'm around. That is why I am taking myself away from here. I will be in Moldova soon and I shall live as I did when I was under the spell of the master. I don't care about anyone there, but I don't want to hurt you. I will try to find out what Dimitri's concoction was and then I hope to return to you. Promise you'll wait for me.

Your love,
Ludmila.

When I finished the note, I crunched it up in my hand and stared out the window. I looked at the trees and clouds and

66

wondered where she was at that moment. Suddenly, it struck me how absurd- the whole thing was. I asked myself, was it possible to love a vampire and live a normal life at the same time? What had I done? Was I sinning? I did love her very much but now she was gone from me. I wanted her back, but I wanted her to come back of her own accord. I was not going to seek her out. I resolved to try and forget her and Moldova and everything to do with my time spent there. It would not be easy and I didn't relish the idea of life without my Ludmila. Something told me to try and make a new life for myself and perhaps with somebody else. Somebody who was mortal. My mind was in a terrible place. I would meet someone else and I would tell them how I was deserted by one who I thought, loved me. I had been deluded, not thinking straight. I vowed to get my house in order. I would marry again. I am now putting this journal away and forgetting all of this. My life will be different from now on.

End of journal.

I looked at Ellen and she looked back at me. I don't think we knew what to say to each other at the time. We heard a noise in the hall; it was Ellen's parents arriving home. She grabbed the diary from me and pushed it under a cushion on the sofa. She then sat on it.

"Not a word about it." she whispered with her finger against her lips. The door opened and her father came in. He came over, shook my hand and said how glad he was to see me again. He wanted to know what I was doing with myself these days. I was telling him about working in the bookshop when suddenly Ellen burst in, "Dad, where is my great, great grandfather buried?"

"He's buried in St Mary's churchyard with his wife and family. It's a family vault. I'm surprised you've never been there. I don't think they lock the gate in the evening so you should still get in. Don't let it get too late or you won't be able to see where you're going. Ah, I know why you're asking. It's this ghost thing that you've gotten into your head. I suppose,

John, you've heard all about this. It's been going on for weeks, Ellen's hearing things." He laughed. "The sound of music and noises in the night. Do you think she could be a writer someday, John, with an imagination like that?" He stood up and said he was going to see if there was any tea going. As soon as the door closed behind him, Ellen grabbed the diary from under the cushion and said we were leaving.

"Where to?" I asked.

"St Mary's churchyard. It looks like Daniel married again and had a family. I want to see his grave."

We left the house quietly and drove in the direction of St Mary's churchyard. It wasn't too far. It was an old church still in use with a graveyard all around it. The iron gate made a noise as we went in and overhead the crows made a noisy cawing sound. It didn't take long to find the crypt. It was large and made of grey stone.

"Look at that," said Ellen, "he had a wife and children. He obviously married again and made a new life for himself."

"Can you make the bit in the middle out," I asked, brushing away some ivy that clung to the inscription?

"Hold on for a minute," said Ellen as she strained to read it. "Died from a fall from his horse. So, we know where he's buried, how he died, and that he married again. I don't understand all these strange happenings at home."

"There's nothing more we can do here," I said and walked back towards the car. She hesitated for a moment and then followed me. She got in and banged the door shut.

"What now?" she said.

"I don't know, let's think on it for a while. What are you going to do with the diary?"

"I'm going to put it back in the box in the old nursery where I found it, then again maybe I'll just burn it," she replied. She dropped me home and I asked her if she wanted to come in.

"No, I'm going to go home, have a cup of strong tea and talk to my sisters. I haven't really been talking to them much since all this stuff started happening. Then…" she continued putting her hand on my face, "I intend to get a good night's sleep. Good luck with your Dad."

"I can telephone you tomorrow evening, that is if you'd like me to," I said.

"Yeah, that would be lovely," she replied. We kissed and I got out. She started the engine and sped off. I looked after the car until it disappeared out of sight and then went inside to face my parent's curiosity.

Chapter 11

"John is that you?" I recognised the voice of our neighbour's son, Patrick Kelly. I thought it strange to hear his voice in the house and not those of my parents. I rushed into the sitting room. Patrick was sitting there on his own, looking very serious.

"What's wrong, where's Mam and Dad?" I asked. He looked down at the floor and then back up at me.

"Your father had some sort of turn; they think it might be his heart. He went in the ambulance about half an hour ago. Your mother went with him." I was shocked but felt in control at the same time. There's something in us that takes over at these times of crisis.

"Can you drop me over to the hospital, Pat?" I asked.

"Of course, get your coat." I got my coat and within seconds we were in Patrick's car. He wound up the engine and the car came to life. He jumped in and we sped off in the direction of St Philomena's. We didn't speak much along the way and suddenly, Ellen's face appeared in my mind's eye. It was a very lonely feeling that came on me after I'd heard the news about Dad. I was glad I knew Ellen at this time.

It didn't take too long to get there and I jumped out feeling awful.

"Do you want me to come with you?" asked Patrick. I knew his heart was going out to me.

"No," I said, "thanks for everything. Go home and have a cup of tea. I'll let you know how it all goes." He shook my hand and I watched him driving away. I went to the reception and asked where Dad was.

"Thomas Wilson is in the casualty unit," said receptionist looking up a long list. "He's still unconscious. It appears he's had some sort of a heart attack. If you make your way down to the end of that corridor over there and turn left, you'll be at casualty." I rushed down the pale green coloured corridor and turned to the left as she'd said. I went straight to the woman at the desk and asked for Thomas Wilson and told her that I was his son. She called a nurse who just happened to pass through and told her who I was. The nurse gave me a sympathetic smile and told me to follow her. She said that she didn't know a lot about my dad as she was not involved in his care but would take me to him. I walked beside her and remember feeling it was the longest walk I'd ever done.

"In there," said the nurse. I pushed my way in through a heavy white door with a spring on it. There were several people standing around the walls and sitting in chairs. I saw Mam at the end of Dad's bed. She was crying and a nurse was trying to comfort her. I walked over to where she was and put my arm around her shoulder.

"Oh John, thank God you're here," she sobbed. I looked at Dad and he was very still and pale in the bed. I started to feel the urge to cry but tried to contain myself. I touched his arm which was out over the blanket, it was freezing. I covered it up.

"He hasn't woken up," she said. "The doctor said he was hopeful but time will tell. Say your prayers, John." I sat down and told her to go and get a cup of tea. She didn't want to, but I insisted. They'd been married a long time and always did everything together. I hoped they were going to get through this together too. I looked at Dad and there wasn't a move out of him. I began to wonder was he still with us. He looked as if he was not real. I started to see images in my mind of when I was a child, and all the things, I had done with him. The thought of him not waking up again was dreadful. I couldn't bear to think about it.

After about twenty minutes, Mam came back and asked me if there had been any change. I told her no. She told me to go home and get some rest and that she would call me if Dad woke up. I said that I'd sit in the visitor's room for a while. I got up and made my way in the direction of the visitor's room; it was close by. There were blinds on the windows with a small red sofa and some chairs. I was the only one there and sat down on the sofa. I looked at a magazine that was on a small table, but I couldn't concentrate on anything. I flicked through the pages and then left it down again. Suddenly, the door opened and a nurse was standing there.

"If you want to come with me," she said, "your dad has woken up and is asking for you." I ran down the corridor ahead of her. She called after me telling me to slow down and not excite my father as he was still feeling very weak. When I got there, Dad was still lying down but awake. He was holding Mam's hand. As soon as he saw me his face became anxious and I hurried towards him.

"Dad, oh Dad you're alright again, you've woken up." He tried to shake my hand which I had offered to him but there was no strength in his grip.

"Don't cry Mam," I said as my mother put her head down.

"I can't help it," she replied. "I don't know if it's shock or relief, but who cares, your Dad is going to be alright." Dad winked at me and I wasn't sure what he meant. He winked again and made a signal that he wanted to talk to me alone. I managed to get Mam to go for a break in the family room and have a cup of tea. I would stay with Dad for a while. She was reluctant to go, but I managed to get around her. I closed the door behind her and I could see Dad was peppering to tell me.

"What is it?" I asked, "For God's sake don't get worked up now. You've got to take it slowly."

"I had an experience that I need to tell you about." He struggled to get the words out.

"Don't strain yourself," I said feeling concerned about him.

"Listen to me," he continued getting annoyed, "I had one of those out of body experiences. For God's sake don't tell your mother or she'll think my brain was affected as well. It concerns you and Ellen." I looked at him with growing interest and wondered what he was going to come out with.

He told me to draw my chair nearer to him. I also checked to make sure there was no sign of Mam.

"I'm all ears Dad, go on what happened," I said feeling excited. He cleared his throat, looked slowly around him and said,

"You and Ellen Rackley are in some sort of danger. It was like you were walking in to a room and there was a figure watching you in the background. It felt as if I was looking at a wild animal waiting to pounce, but it wasn't an animal, it was human. I didn't see enough details, but it felt frightening." He gripped my arm, "Be careful son. I know people would find it hard to believe, but I know what I saw." My mother suddenly arrived back and sat down.

"The doctor said it looks like a heart attack but that you seem to be doing okay," she smiled as she said this and pressed on his arm in a reassuring way. "They say you'll probably be here for a few days, maybe even a week. You were unconscious for a while so they want to keep an eye on you."

"I'm alright, don't worry about me," said Dad. I could already see the light coming back into his eye. Suddenly, there was knock at the door and turning around we saw Ellen coming through. She told us Patrick Kelly had told her what happened when she rang on the telephone looking to talk to me. She kissed my parents on the cheek and sat down on the end of the bed.

"You were very good to come Ellen," said Mam.

"Not at all Mrs Wilson, glad to see you smiling Mr Wilson."

"I'll always manage a smile when you're around Ellen," said Dad. We stayed for a little while longer and Ellen said she'd give us a lift home. Mam said she wanted to talk to the doctor on the way out and told us to go ahead to the car. The doctor came in to the room and started talking to Mam and Dad. Ellen and I left and went outside to the cold and dark night. We got in and sat there not saying anything. I couldn't think of anything except Dad. Ellen sat silently probably wondering what to say. It was me that broke the silence.

"Thanks for coming. It was very nice of you. Mam was delighted to see you."

"No, not at all," she said placing her hand on my arm.

"Why did you ring the house?" I asked.

"I couldn't rest. When I got home, I sat downstairs for a while and then went to my bedroom. I decided to read a bit, but I couldn't concentrate. I felt someone or something was there watching me. When I couldn't stand it any longer, I decided to call you and it was then that Patrick told me what had happened. I felt terrible for you all." Before I got a chance to say anything, Mam arrived back. I thought she looked a bit brighter.

"He's going to be in hospital for a week maybe more. The doctor said it was a good sign that he woke up and that he's talking but that he is very weak."

"Let's go home Mam," and short time later we arrived at home.

Chapter 12

Ellen dropped us home and promised she'd ring tomorrow to see how Dad was. Mam went in ahead of me and I sat with Ellen for a few minutes.

"I know this happening to your Dad changes things," she said looking out in to the darkness.

"Of course," I replied, "but he'll get better. He told me something happened to him when he was unconscious. He had a vision or something of us being in danger and told me to be careful. I can't tell Mam; she might think his mind has become affected."

"We know what's true, don't we?" she asked.

"Do we?" I replied. "It's all strange and hard to believe." I noticed a look had come on her face and I felt she didn't like me saying that. She started the engine and said she'd be in touch. We had a short kiss and before I knew it, she was driving away.

When I went into the sitting room, my mother was sitting on an armchair drinking a cup of tea. She glanced around when she heard me coming in.

"Ah, there you are, is Ellen gone?" she asked with a knowing look on her face.

"Yeah, she's gone. She's very nice and a good friend," My mother smiled.

"What?" I asked.

"Oh nothing. You're right, she is a nice girl. You're seeing a lot of her lately. It was nice of her to come and see your father. I get a feeling there's something going on between you. As I said, she's very nice."

"Okay Mam!" I said sitting down, "I do like her and yes we have been spending time together. She does have some concerns though and I'm helping her with them."

"What sort of concerns?"

"Promise not to laugh if I tell you."

"No, I won't laugh. I don't know when I'll laugh again, after what's happened to your father." A tear came to her eye and to mine too. I put my arm around her.

"I'm okay John," she said, "Dad will be back with us probably soon and in the meantime, we'll visit him every day and look forward to him coming home. You've got me all curious about Ellen, what sort of concerns does she have?"

"She's frightened. She heard strange noises at night. She thinks there's a ghost in her house. I think there's something in it." My mother turned her head and looked at me as if I had two heads.

"Now John, listen to me. You've never gone on about ghosts before. If Ellen Rackley is filling your head with nonsense, I'd rather you keep your distance from her. What do you mean you think there's something in it? For God's sake, would you have sense?"

"You forget Mam," I replied, "I stayed there for a night and I heard and saw strange things."

"What sort of things?" she asked with a mystified look on her face.

"I don't know, I don't know just strange feelings or something. There's a history to the house, maybe that has something to do with it."

"All these big houses have history, so what? In fact, every house has history."

"You always have a way of bringing things back to normal," I replied. "I'm going to bed. I'll see you in the morning." I left her there and went up to my bedroom. She raised her eyes as I walked out of the room. I got undressed and ready for bed. I didn't feel like sleeping. I kept thinking of Dad in hospital and wondering how he was and what was he thinking. Then my mind switched to Ellen and I wondered if she was alright. I sat on the bed drinking a glass of milk that

I'd brought up with me. I got to thinking about Daniel Rackley and his diary. I wondered what sort of man he was. It was all so unbelievable. I lay down to sleep and set the clock for seven in the morning, as I had to go to work. Despite my restless feelings and my mind working overtime, I managed to sleep well.

Chapter 13

The phone ringing in the hall woke me up. I looked at my watch; it was only twelve o' clock, a little over an hour after I'd gone to bed. I lit a candle and hurried downstairs. I held the bannister tightly as I was still half asleep. I could hear Mam stirring in her room. I picked up the receiver and said hello. It was Ellen's father and he sounded troubled.

"Is that John?" he said in a loud voice.

"Yes, oh hello Mr Rackley, is everything alright?"

"Is Ellen with you?"

"No," I replied, "she left me off at about half ten. Is there something wrong?" He didn't reply for a few seconds and I thought I heard a cry in his voice.

"I'm going out to look for her and I wondered would you do the same. I know it's late, but I thought maybe you might have some idea of where she could be, you know, favourite places of where you both like to go. My wife and I are worried, we're going to call the guards, but we wanted to see if you knew anything, as you were the last person to see her." I couldn't help feeling his words had an accusing ring to them, but I also knew that I could be very sensitive at times. It had been a torment to me in life, but I was determined to get out of it someday.

"I know she took the road by the church home instead of taking the direct route," I replied. "She's got an interest in the church, though I can't see what would bring her there this time of night."

"Can you get a lend of your father's car?" he asked in a voice that sounded like he was desperate. I told him I could and that I would take the road to the church as I could get there quicker. He said he'd take the other way and maybe we'd meet up at the church. He hung up suddenly and I raced upstairs to put my shoes and dressing gown on. Mam was at the top of the stairs with her hand to her mouth.

"I heard what you said, oh God I hope nothing's happened to Ellen." I hurried past her and with my heart racing, I got ready as quick as I could. She told me to be careful as I ran back down the stairs, grabbed the car keys from the hook in the hall and shouted back that I needed to borrow Dad's car.

"Just be careful," she said loudly. I ran to the garage and threw the doors open. I started the car up with a few winds. It spluttered and roared and I drove out into the black night.

The night was very dark and the big trees along the road made it even darker. I drove on for what seemed like ages, but it wasn't really. I saw the steeple of the church sticking up over the trees like a black spike. On coming around the corner I spotted Ellen's car. It was at the gate of the church with the driver's door opened. I pulled in behind it and jumped out. There was no sign of her. The church gate was opened and I ran in among the graves that surrounded the church. It was very silent. I called Ellen's name several times, but there was no reply. I walked around to the side of the church and spotted a shape in the dark lying on the grave of her great, great grandfather. I ran towards it and saw it was Ellen. I knelt and shook her. There was no response. I called her name but still nothing came from a very silent Ellen. The moon came out from behind a cloud and by its dull grey light, I spotted two marks like bites on her neck and a small trail of blood coming from them. With all we'd been talking about lately and having read about vampires, I could see what had happened or thought, *I could anyway*. I ran inside the porch of the church which was left open at night and filled a small container there with holy water. I rushed back and poured the water on the wounds. It seemed to burn her and suddenly opening her eyes, she screamed. The marks on her neck just disappeared. She sat up and suddenly realising she was sitting on her ancestor's grave, she asked me to help her to her feet. I got her up and she was shaking from head to toe. She looked around her in a confused manner. "What happened?" she asked. I told her about her car being outside the church and finding her here lying on the grave.

"I don't remember everything," she said sobbing. "I do remember leaving you and then someone on the road in front of the car. I remember feeling cold and a strange kind of sting in my neck." She felt her neck but all trance of the marks were gone. I heard a car coming near the church and I guessed it to be her parents.

"Ellen," I said, "you've had an encounter with whatever it is that's in your house. Tell your parents you felt faint, got out to have a walk and must have fainted. They'll be just glad to have you safe."

"Ellen, Ellen." her mother and father were calling to her as their car pulled up at the gate to the church. They hurried from the car and embraced her. She told them what I had told her to say. They thanked me and told me to call later tomorrow after they'd gotten the doctor to check over Ellen. They all three walked away and as they were going through the gate, Ellen looked back. I waved and they got into their car and drove away. I stood there and looked at the grave of Daniel Rackley. I thought to myself, *Daniel Rackley, you have a lot to answer for*.

Chapter 14

The following morning, I was up and getting ready for work. I was on my way downstairs when I heard the telephone ringing. I stopped to listen as I heard Mam answering it.

"Oh, hello Ellen, I didn't expect to hear your voice on the phone this hour of the morning. I thought after your little ordeal last night, you'd probably be still asleep." There was a short pause and then I heard Mam's voice again.

"Dad is doing okay. I rang the hospital very early this morning and they said he had a good night. Thanks for asking and for the lift last night but never mind us, just get strong again and mind yourself." There was another pause and I waited for Mam's voice again.

"John, yes, he's here. He's only just up but I heard his step on the stairs a minute ago." I arrived into the kitchen and she handed me the telephone.

"It's Ellen," she whispered, "she must have it bad to be ringing you at this hour of the morning."

"Would you stop please!" I said taking the telephone from her. I picked up the earpiece and I could hear her breathing quickly.

"Hello, Ellen. Is everything alright?" I asked. There was no answer for a few seconds and they she spoke rapidly.

"John, can you meet me for lunch today? It would be better if you could try and make it a long lunch. I need you to be with me now, more than ever. I had a strange dream after I left you last night, well I think it was more than a dream. Mam and Dad called the doctor and he came late last night. He gave me something to sooth me and said I was possibly suffering from some sort of stress or strain and that these things can affect our minds. He asked me was there anything bothering me but no way was I going to tell him about, you know what. He said blackouts and sleep walking can be put down to tension and I'm to take it easy for a few days. I feel okay today, but I need to meet you."

"Okay!" I answered, "When and where do you want to meet or is it alright for you to drive after what's happened?" I could detect she was a bit annoyed with me asking this and told me that she wasn't an invalid.

"I'll collect you from work at one o' clock and we can go to Morton's," she said, "I'll talk to you there. Is that okay with you?"

"Yeah, that's fine. Okay at one then." The phone went dead suddenly. She really seemed frightened, I thought. There was no use speculating. I hung up and went back into the kitchen. I wanted to see her at that very minute. I didn't feel I could wait until lunch time.

"Why was Ellen on the telephone so early?" Mam asked. I didn't answer for a few seconds, I couldn't. I imagined Ellen sitting in a corner, somewhere in that big house and crying.

"Well John, what did she want, is everything alright? Is she recovered after last night?"

"Just wanted to know if I'd like to meet her for lunch, that's all. They got the doctor for her. She's to take it easy, it's nothing serious."

"Oh well," Mam replied, "that's good if she feels up to lunch. You know son, you might just end up living in that big old house yet. If you're heading into work, I'll drive you in. I'm going in to see your dad this morning. Will I tell him you'll be in later?"

"Yeah," I said, "that would be great." I sat down and tucked into my breakfast. Mam was rambling on about the tap in the kitchen giving problems and how Dad would have had it fixed if he was here now. She got a bit tearful and then spoke about how the back garden needed a job done on it. I could hear what she was saying but my mind was on Ellen, Daniel, and Ludmila. I knew I should be thinking of Dad, but I felt satisfied that he was out of danger. I didn't feel the same about

Ellen and her face kept coming to mind. I wondered what had happened. *Was there something evil in the house? Did it mean to harm Ellen or her family? How come none of them have not felt there was something wrong in the house? What could we do about it? Should we tell anyone about the diary?* All these questions were going around in my head. My distraction was broken by a spoon falling from the table. Mam smiled at me. "Ah, you're back with us. Now what could be on your mind? Let me see, could it be Ellen Rackley?" We both laughed.

"Come on," she said, "get your coat and I'll wait for you in the car." I grabbed my coat from the hall and followed her out to the car. She handed me the starting handle and I gave the engine a windup. I jumped in and we rattled away towards town. There was a spot along the way where it was possible to see a part of Ellen's home through the trees. I strained to see it and Mam laughed at me. I sat back in silence, embarrassed.

"How is Ellen about all that spooky stuff that you told me about?" asked Mam. I didn't like her asking me, I felt she was making a laugh of Ellen even though I knew she wasn't really. I didn't answer and Mam didn't say anything else for the remainder of the short journey.

She dropped me at the corner just down from the bookshop where I worked.

"Thanks Mam!" I said as I opened the door to get out. "Tell Dad I'll come in to see him later."

"See you later." and kissing me on the cheek, she drove off without delay. I walked up the street and looked around at how peaceful and normal everything seemed at that early hour. I couldn't imagine anyone believing what Ellen was saying. I did see that diary though and I believed it, even if it went against anything I would believe. I arrived at the tell-tale and the bell rang over the door, as I walked in. I hung up my coat and asked Susan if Mr Maguire was in.

"Yeah, he's in his office, why do you want to know?" she asked. I told her I needed to take a long lunch.

"He seems in okay humour so go ahead and ask. Muriel is here all day so we should be fine for a few hours." Susan was the type of person that saw the best in everyone. I knocked at the door of the office and I heard Mr Maguire saying, "Come in." I entered and found him sitting at his desk writing something. He didn't look up and kept on writing for another two minutes or so. Eventually he put down the pen and asked me what I wanted. I explained, I needed to take a long lunch, and would it be alright to do so.

"Yes, I think we're covered today, staff wise. How long more are you going to stay here?" he asked. The question was like a bolt out of the blue.

"Are you not happy with my performance here, Mr Maguire?" I asked. He laughed out loud.

"Don't be silly, I'm more than happy with you and although you do a fair days' work, I suspect your heart is not quite in it. You know more about books besides selling them. Go and teach others about them. Think about it, maybe it's your time." The telephone on his desk rang and I took that as my cue to leave. As I shut the door behind me, I couldn't help thinking about what he'd said. Maybe it was time to teach and keep company with Ellen Rackley. Maybe, I thought, my life was changing.

Chapter 15

One o' clock came around quick enough and I spotted Ellen's car outside the shop. I said goodbye to Susan and Muriel and told them I'd be back late. I could see them straining at the window, trying to get a glimpse of who was driving away with me. Ellen was wearing a red scarf and hat and she smiled at me as I got in.

"Have you been waiting here long?" I asked.

"No, just arrived, are you ready to go?"

"Let's go," I said. The engine spluttered and we drove down the main street towards Morton's. Ellen was quiet and I asked her if something was wrong.

"I'll talk to you when we get to Morton's," she said.

A little while later we arrived and made out way into the cosy little pub. We ordered tea and chips. She was nervous and jumpy.

"Had you any trouble getting a long lunch break?" she asked.

"No," I replied, "none at all. Have your chips first and then we'll talk." The tea and chips arrived and we munched into them.

"I can't really wait any longer to tell you," she said.

"I'm listening. You said it was some sort of dream that seemed to be more than a dream."

"It was. You're not going to believe me. After the doctor left last night, I went straight to bed and fell asleep quickly. I thought I began to dream but now I'm not sure if it was a dream. It was so frightening and real."

"Go on" I said, "what happened next?"

"I felt the blankets were slowly being pulled off me. I thought I looked up from the pillow and you can imagine the terror I felt when I saw, who I took to be, Ludmila standing at the end of my bed. I couldn't scream. I froze and all my muscles seemed to tense up. She put her finger to her lips as a sign for me to stay quiet. Her finger nail was long and pointed.

'I am Ludmila. You know that, don't you?' she asked with a commanding air. 'You know that of course, you know all about me, you know what I am and what I can do. You were very close to joining me tonight but here you are in what used to be my house. I lived here for a short time with an ancestor of yours. He loved me and I loved him. How much do you know?' she asked fiercely, flashing her sharp white fangs. I managed to find my voice again and I told her about the diary and that I knew about everything.

'I returned to Moldova because I knew I would hurt him and his loved ones when I no longer had Dimitri's mixture. I fled after his death and returned to my old ways of preying on human victims. Daniel, your great, great grandfather, quickly forgot about me and was able to marry again. I felt hurt by that.' She stopped and I waited for her to say something else. I didn't have long to wait and she glided nearer to me. I felt terrified but in a kind of shock that prevented me from shouting or crying.

'I have since found Dimitri's recipe,' she began, 'and I do not have to attack humans anymore. A change has come on me, of late. I no longer want to live on. I'm not really living anyway. I want you to release my soul from this living nightmare. If you refuse me this request, I shall come in the night and make you one of the undead and your beloved John and all your family. I nearly had you already, don't forget that. You will have no peace ever again if you do not do as I say.'." Ellen was starting to shake as she told me this. I found it impossible to believe.

"I can't believe I'm hearing this," I said, "it can't be anything more than a bad dream."

"There's more," said Ellen, "hear me out. Ludmila is in the house. She has told me where she is and what she wants me to do to release her from this terrible existence. I need you to help me."

"What exactly would that involve? I've heard of wooden stakes being put through the hearts of vampires, but I don't think I want to be involved in any of that."

"Listen!" said Ellen with a firmness in her voice. "Ludmila is in our attic. It has a large window or skylight in the ceiling which has a thick heavy screen across it, blocking out the light. This is opened and shut by a long cord that hangs down. I've only ever been in the attic once and nobody ever goes there. Ludmilla told me about wandering the house at night and staring up sadly at the black night sky through the glass when the daylight has gone. There is a heavy curtain in the attic and she rests under it during the day. She wants us to place her directly under the skylight and then hopefully the daylight will do its job. Will you help me now today to do it?"

"Yes." I answered with some hesitation in my voice, hoping I would wake from this nightmare.

"Let's finish here and go back to my house. I'll smuggle you in the back way and then we'll make our way to the attic. Don't think I'm not afraid." she continued noticing my reluctance. I looked at her and said,

"If you can do it, I can do it."

We walked outside into what was a bright sunny day in which a dark business was to take place. We got into the car and I ducked down in the back seat. As the car bumped and rattled along, I had to keep reminding myself this wasn't murder. Ludmila had been dead for a long time but she was trapped through no fault of her own. She must be released or it would be bad for all of us.

Chapter 16

A while later, Ellen's car came to a halt. She got out and told me to wait for a minute and that she would go and see if the coast was clear. After what seemed like eternity but was only about five minutes, she came back. She opened the door of the car at the same time telling me to get out quickly. She led me in through the back door and we stopped in the kitchen while she checked to see if it was safe to go on. I thought of the night we sat there and talked; it was a pleasant memory. She waved her hand and beckoned for me to follow her. There was a horrible feel to it all. We made our way to Ellen's bedroom and closed the door behind us.

"Can you stay quiet if I leave you for a few minutes?" she asked.

"Of course, I can." I answered feeling slightly annoyed by her question, "Why do you ask?"

"I want to check that it's all clear up to the attic. We must walk up a corridor and turn at the end."

"Go ahead then," I said, "I won't make a sound. You can trust me, you know."

"Thank you!" said Ellen giving me a little smile and trying to make me feel in better humour again. She turned the brass door knob very slowly and shut the door behind her as she went out. I sat on her large iron bed and tried not to make a sound. The image of what we came to do flashed across my mind and I began to dread it, even more than I had already. I thought to myself, *how big the world was and here I was sitting on a bed waiting to end a life*. I wondered *how I'd found myself here.*

About ten minutes later, Ellen came back and again closed the door slowly behind her. She sat beside me on the bed and asked if I was ready to act. I told her I had thought so but now felt afraid.

"Don't back out on me now," she said. "I need you there." I thought I detected a sound of panic in her voice. I took a deep breath, "Come on," I said, "let's bring this thing to an end."

"That's the spirit!" she replied and took my hand as we left the bedroom and again closed the door gently behind us. We walked slowly along a long corridor with a red carpet. With every step I took, I felt my heart beating faster. I could hear movement and voices that seemed to come from way off in the other side of the house. The sounds and voices seemed to travel along the corridors and through the house. There was a lonely feel to it.

"That's Dillon and Mary you hear," said Ellen, "they're the only ones here now. They're used to me coming in and out and wandering around the house, so we shouldn't have any interference from them." We turned a corner and there was a door in front of us with four steps leading up to it.

"That's the attic," said Ellen, "we can walk in." I nodded back to her as I couldn't speak with the fear that was now growing inside me. She turned the large key in the door and it made a noisy clunk sound as the lock shot back. I looked around the corner but all seemed quiet. Ellen turned the handle and the door opened. It was stiff from not being used and made a terrible squeaking sound. We went in and closed it behind us. Above our heads was a large window or type of skylight in the roof. It had a heavy blind across it that was blocking out the daylight. I looked up at it and then at Ellen. She nodded as if she'd read my thought and said,

"Yes, let's do this thing." I pulled the long cord that led to the blind and it rose up letting the sunlight come shining in. The particles of dust could be seen flying around in its rays. In the far corner there was what looked like a heavy black or dark blue curtain. We approached it slowly and could see there was a shape under it, the shape of a person. I began to shake from head to foot. I had never felt fear like this in my life.

"Can you do this?" I whispered. Ellen nodded her head and between us we pushed the shape under the skylight. I went to remove the curtain, but she stopped me.

"Let me do it," she said. I watched as the curtain, covered in dirt, was dragged slowly away. Under it lay an extremely pale but beautiful young woman dressed in a white dress with long dark hair. It was the same woman I had seen when I arrived for Ellen's party. Her mouth was closed and I couldn't see anything of the sharp teeth that we'd read about. The sunlight on her face made her look even paler and her long slender arms were by her sides. Her eyes started to twitch and open slowly and she looked with difficulty at the blue sky above her through the skylight. She said in a deep foreign accent,

"Ah, peace at last!" and then vanished from our sight in a cloud or mist which seemed to come out of nowhere.